Kernik looked at his hands,

bloodless white as the stone of the quarry. He smiled and put on them rings of silver and gold. He dressed his body in a robe the shade of storms, embroidered twenty times with the face of the sun. He looked back at the black rubble which had been the statue of Takerna. Then he glanced about where the sun was pouring, searching for something which he did not find.

Kernik no longer cast a shadow.

Kernik raised his arms. They were wings. Lifted his head. It was a bird's cruel hooked mask. Kernik was a falcon, and the falcon flew up into the air and screamed derisively.

More than illusion now, it was reality. For Kernik flew with feathers on his back, Kernik-Takerna-Volk flew with the sun in his sideways eyes, high over the husk of the black god and the humility of the golden land, and the magician Volkhavaar was born.

VOLKHAVAAR

Tanith Lee

DAW BOOKS, INC.
Donald A. Wollheim, Publisher

1633 Broadway
New York, N.Y. 10019

DEDICATION:

Quietly

to

R.

FIRST PRINTING, JULY 1977

3 4 5 6 7 8 9

 DAW TRADEMARK REGISTERED
U.S. PAT. OFF. MARCA
REGISTRADA. HECHO EN U.S.A.

PRINTED IN U.S.A.

VOLKHAVAAR

"Love is a ring,
and a ring has no end."

—Russian proverb

PART ONE

The Slave Girl
and Her Heart

* 1 *

The sun in his golden chariot had driven almost to the last meadow of the sky. Presently, the six yellow horses who pulled him would snort the rose-pink smoke from their nostrils, and gallop behind the horizon. Then the twilight would come like a dark widow and throw her veil across the heaven and the earth, but long before she did, Shaina, the slave would be back in the valley below with her master's goats.

Shaina did not take the goats up to the mountain pasture every day in the spring. Young Ash, the master's son, was supposed to do it, but Young Ash got drunk every fourth or fifth night, and so every fifth or sixth day, while Young Ash lay groaning under his bearskin blanket, invoking all the demons of the house to have pity on him, Old Ash's wife would call the slave and send the goats with her.

Shaina was never displeased at this task. Her owners did not like her to sit idle on the slope, and gave her the washing and the mending to take with her, which meant a heavy basket to carry up and down on her back. She must keep both eyes on, and both hands ready for the goats, who in goat fashion were all mad, and anxious to prove themselves so. Nevertheless, it was good on the mountain, sprinkled with the little flowers of spring and alive with the rushing silver of streams swollen in the thaw. The surrounding peaks were very close, each with its own shape and color, yet all continually changing under the moods of the sky, now dagger bright as the light sharpened them, now transparent with mist and distance, and now like stationary clouds. To the village, every height had a character and a name—Elf Roof, Cold Crag, Black Top. Some were blessed, some feared. But, whatever else, to sit working in their shadow was far better certainly than to be shut in the sooty house, among Old Ash's wife and the cook-pots with, for variety, the shouting dog in the yard, and the

children who threw pebbles at her. Generally, after a day
on the slopes, Shaina would return refreshed, almost glad-
dened, to the village.

Yet this sunset, as she came down the winding stony
track, basket on back, goats milling about her and the air
like a song, there was growing in the slave a curious
melting sadness.

It did not come as a stranger to her, this melancholy.
For the past ten months it had approached and withdrawn,
each time a fraction nearer, a fraction sweeter and more
bitter in her heart. Shaina found she could give it no
name.

It was not the harsh, grim sorrow of her slavery; she
had grown used to that. Strong and proud and young she
was; she had come very quickly to courage and determination: 'I will not be slave forever, and if I am to be a
slave, I will hold my head higher even than the Duke's
daughter at Arkev.'

Dark cruel men had snatched her from her home when
she was six years old. She could remember little now of
that wild passage, smoke and fire behind, terror before. A
great sea had flung their ships on to a rocky shore, and
she had come in chains and barefoot, with bleeding soles
and weeping eyes, to the Korkeem, the place where she
was to grow. Here she forgot her country, all but a ghost
of it, only the voices of her ancestors, her race, reminded
her, and sometimes her dreams. Her land was warm and
this land cold, but this cold land became her land, and its
ways, her ways, because she could recall no others. Only
her pride she kept, the heritage that was somehow part of
her bones and could not desert her. And though she was
Old Ash's slave, she had not been his slave always, and
had seen more of her adopted world than the villagers
who walked freely. At seven she had been sold, and again
at ten, and into Old Ash's service when she was sixteen.
Journeying between these slave markets, she had observed
three villages and one town, and even passed near the
sun-and-moon city of Arkev, where the Duke ate roasted
swans in a white palace whose every tower had a hat of
yellow metal. Old Ash and Old Ash's wife had ventured
perhaps as far as Kost on market day. As for Young Ash,
the tavern over the hill in the next village was the farthest
he had ever been.

So Shaina had her pride, her travelled superiority, a

little homesickness, and much resilience, and thus did not understand the sadness that came at sunset on the mountain.

A mirror, maybe, might have taught her, but the bronze mirror in the house was warped and dull, and besides, a slave had little time for such looking. A stream might have taught her, if it had stood still long enough to be a mirror, but the streams of the Korkeem were always busy rushing and ruffling in the spring, and in the winter frozen to marble. Her hair was shining black as midnight with stars in it and long and thick as the tails of horses, her eyes were the color of oak leaves in autumn an hour before the wind gives them wings. She was straight and slim, and she did not look like a slave nor walk like one. Indeed, perhaps the Duke in sky-worshipping Arkev would have been pleased to see his clumsy daughter carry herself as Shaina did, basket and goats and all.

There was a point, quite far down the slopes, where the track ran round a big rock. In the side of this rock someone had carved, centuries before, the image of a demon or a mountain deity, which the villagers always politely addressed when passing. Shaina, too, had got into the habit of nodding to the idol, and wishing it good-day or good-evening, for in this country of devils, sprites and goblins, you could not be too careful. The goats also behaved oddly when they went by, bleating and butting worse than usual. This sunset, however, reaching the rock, they all abruptly bunched together and fell uncharacteristically silent, rolling their eyes. Shaina looked up, nevertheless, to say her expected phrase to the carving, and it seemed to her that somehow it had a more definite appearance than usual, as if it had mislaid some of its years. But she dismissed this fancy, spoke her greeting, and tried to urge the goats on. When they would not budge, she pushed a way through them and emerged on the other side of the rock.

The sky was gradually darkening now and it was chill, but in the shadowy evocative grey-rose light the slopes were empty and the lamps of the village beginning to appear below. Only one thing was changed; a small boulder, which must have rolled down from higher up, had lodged itself in the middle of the track.

"See," Shaina said to the goats, "it's only a stone. Is it a stone you're afraid of, silly ones?"

The goats shook their beards at her and kept otherwise quite still.

"Don't you know," said Shaina, "that when the night comes over the mountains the dwarfs will pop from holes and carry you off?"

But the goats stared her out, and presently Shania thought she would have to move the terrible boulder. So she walked up to it briskly, to show the goats there was nothing to fear. Just then the boulder gave a sort of shift and a lift and turned its head and looked at her out of two black eyes.

Shaina stopped still herself at that, but she said nothing since it seemed wiser to remain silent.

" 'Not everything that walks is a man,' " said the boulder conversationally, " 'and not everything that lies quiet is a stone,' as the wolf remarked when the serpent bit him."

"So I see," said Shaina.

And so she did, for the boulder was none other than a strange grey-looking old woman in a mossy bundle of shawl, with a puckered grey old face and eyes like black knife points poking through it.

"You are the slave from the village," said the old woman. "You have crossed other soil than this and drawn water from other wells. You are ready for something. Do you know for what?"

"I am ready to go back to my master's house, Mother, or I shall be beaten."

"The rod strikes the back not the heart," said the old woman implacably. "Your heart, my fine high and mighty slave girl, is ready to be hurt. You stand there as if you carried velvet on your back instead of washing, and had silver rings on your ankles. I tell you, before tomorrow is over and done, you'll come like a beggar to me, and offer me the blood in your veins and the marrow in your bones, in exchange for my help."

Shaina felt herself go pale, for she was frightened by the old woman, not so much her peculiar words as the way she said them and the quite inexplicable expression on her face. But when Shaina was afraid, something like iron came into her. She answered firmly.

"If I am to come begging your help, then who shall I say I seek?"

"Ask in the village, slave maiden. Ask anyone. Tell them you met a stone that talked on the mountain, and that the stone was grey and it had black eyes. And now, you and your goats may pass on. Look, there is the way." Shaina looked irresistibly where the old woman pointed. The dark was coming down into the valley like wine into a bowl, and the lights blazed from the narrow windows of the houses. Then it seemed the houses were in motion and the lights flying like yellow bees from one window to another. Shaina's eyes dazzled, her head sang, and the mountain danced under her feet. "Ask in the village who it is that lives westwards on Cold Crag. And then find a bandage for your heart, since before the night is quite finished, someone's look will go straight through it like a sword."

All the goats began to bleat and thrust at Shaina. She caught hold of their rough backs to steady herself, and their golden eyes flashed in a great circle. Next she looked round, and there was no old woman on the track and no boulder either.

"See how foolish it is to stop on the way," said Shaina to the goats. They laughed mournfully. Both they and she knew she had been conversing with a familiar of the mountain.

When she clapped her hands, the goats ran in a woolly tide for the village, and Shaina ran after them as fast as she was able.

✳ 2 ✳

"Slave, you are late," said Old Ash's wife, straightening up steamily from her cauldron of dumplings.

"I beg your pardon," said Shaina.

The goats were in their pen, but Young Ash had already cursed her for bringing them in at such an hour. He had urgent business, he said, over the hill, and what was a slave worth if she could get nothing done, and he cuffed her to teach her to be better. In the yard, the dog looked up from a bone and barked noisily as if to say: "Here comes Shaina, get out the stick!." The dog, who was also in his way a slave, liked to see a human receive the same brutal treatment that he did. But Old Ash was not back yet from the fields, so the wife caught her a clip round the ear to be going on with.

It was indeed quite late. The magic time when the first fires of evening were lighted was long past, the bread and spoons were on the table, and the dishes laid out in their proper places for the house demons. Each demon received a portion of the meal, and woebetide any householder in the Korkeem who forgot them. Even the rich must feed their demons. Old Ash said, even in the palace at Arkev there were little silver plates for the purpose. No home would function without them. There was the demon who looked after the timber in the walls, and the demon who lived in the roof and kept out the rain, and the demon who lay under the threshold and warned the family of any disaster by screaming and wailing. One winter night Young Ash had slipped in the snow coming from the inn, and wrenched his knee, and, having dragged himself to the door, lay there wailing and screaming. Old Ash and his wife had been too terrified to go down because they thought it was the threshold demon warning them about something, and their son had almost perished of cold before neighbors came to his rescue. Nevertheless, demons there were. As a rule they kept hidden, and ate their food

14

when the household slept. But sometimes, in the bleak bizarre hour before sunrise, Shaina, curled stoically on a ragged rug by the ashes of the fire, had opened her eyes and glimpsed a shadow, thin and agile as a snake, creeping away into the walls, leaving its empty dish behind it.

Old Ash was soon in.

He glanced at Shaina with a certain pleasure, for not many villagers could afford a slave. Thanks to this proprietary interest, Shaina received adequate sustenance and shelter, and was allowed to share the family bath, after the rest of them had done with it. Old Ash had also kept Young Ash away from her, no easy task when a young man's proudest boast was how many girls he had had between today and last moon-festival. Still, Young Ash feared his father, a big strapping black bear of a man, and perhaps even more his shrill-tongued mother. Property was not to be damaged or, Mother Earth forbid, got with child when there was so much work to be done.

Old Ash's wife set stew before her husband and poured him beer.

"The slave—" she began, but Old Ash cut her short.

"There has been a wolf after the sheep," he said.

"A wolf!" cried his wife.

"It's late for wolves," said Young Ash, who had come in hurriedly for his supper before setting off over the hill.

"There are wolves and there are wolves," said Old Ash dourly. He chewed his dumpling and said: "And Mikli told me Someone has been seen about again, the Grey Lady from Cold Crag."

"It's two years since ever she came near," said Old Ash's wife. "The women used to go to her for charms and spells, but she drove too hard a bargain. Last winter they were saying they saw her fly off in her chair—the birchwood chair, you recall—but maybe she's come back. She's as old as the rock, and as hard."

"She had better not come back," said Young Ash portentously, finishing his food. "The girls would stone her if she did. There's a slut over the hill has a two-headed child because of trying to be rid of it with a charm of Barbayat's."

"Ssh!" snapped his wife. "Naming names gives powers! Don't you know any better?"

"Better a name than a bellyache," said the son manfully, and strode out.

Shaina dropped the dish of loaves she had been carrying from the oven. She did not mean to. All at once the trembling which had got into her at the mention of the lady of Cold Crag had reached her fingers.

The wife started up like a maddened hen, her hand already reaching for the stick. But at that moment there came a noise in the street outside, so rare, so curious, that it stayed the three of them in tableau. Even Young Ash stopped in the yard. It was the sound of horses hooves and of bells and discs striking on bridle and spur: a sound that only the rich made.

"The tax collector!" cried the wife in a panic.

"The priest from Kost," muttered the husband.

'Death,' thought Shaina, and did no know why she had thought it, though her heart, her young heart that the Grey Lady of Cold Crag had mentioned, turned right over in her breast.

Out into the night went Old Ash and his wife. Even the dog strained on his tether. All along the wide crooked street people were coming to stare, lamps in their hands or bits of bread from supper. Shaina did not go into the road, only as far as the doorway, but she still saw.

Black horses, she could not count their number in the odd shifting light the lamps made, seven, nine, thirteen. . . . And riders—how many? Muffled in cloaks like great black wings folded around themselves. Yet the lamps caught highlights on the scarlet cloth of saddles, reins like chains of stars dripping more stars which were bells, the white metal flash and the yellow, and gems like drops of blood and gems like the green eyes of cats.

And then someone came forward, not hurrying, the first rider on the first horse, slowly, but straight into the full glare of the windows. It was not the priest and it was not the tax collector. Some thought it must be the Duke of the Korkeem himself, and said so, but they were mistaken also. What duke would ride the mounain roads in so much splendor, and with so few—seven, nine, thirteen—behind him.

"I am welcome among you," oddly stated the stranger, looking down on the villagers from the height of his black horse. The stranger wore purple, a shade so dark it too was almost black, and on his purple were embroidered twenty golden suns, their rays stitched apparently with rubies. Around his neck was a collar of gold spikes and on his head a tall hat of saffron bound with silver. His countenance you could barely credit, it was so white, as if thickly enamelled. The eyes were rimmed with gold and the mouth crayoned black-red. Inside his mouth burned teeth pointed and sallow as a wolf's, inside the golden lids burned eyes as lividly stagnant as guttering coals. With one long narrow hand he held the jingling reins, in the other a showman's staff of peeled wood with a knob of dark stone at its tip. The fingernails of his hands were each the length of a rat's tail, pointed and lacquered like jet. He glittered in the window-light, and his paint-face turned from east to west. "Do you know me, good people of the valley? You will."

No one spoke. If fear casts shadows, it cast them then and there. Bowels turned cold and breath tripped. The stranger on the black horse smiled.

"Have you never heard a rumor of Kernik, the Clever Showman? Kernik, the Prince of Conjurors, the Master of Acrobats and Actors, the High Priest of Entertainment? Kernik, Lord of the Laugh, Maker of Magic and Stealer of Scenes?"

Kernik snapped his fingers and his nails clacked. He rapped with his staff on the ground and a shower of sparks shot from it. From out of the sparks a bird flew straight up into the star-dusted sky.

A little mutter ran down the street like a spring breeze. Somewhere, two or three dogs set up a howl and then left off.

"Here are my actors," said Kernik, the Clever Showman, Kernik, Maker of Magic, with a gesture of his predatory hand behind him. "The performers of my troupe. Come, children. Dismount, and the kind people will feed us in return for our wonders."

There was immediately a movement among the horses, like a flock of ravens lifting their wings, letting their wings fall. And then, in the midst of them, there seemed to have been a light kindled: a light without color or heat, yet more brilliant than any other in the village, such that the windows were eclipsed and the lamps snuffed out. Such a blaze of jewels and metal sprang up in that new light that it was like a bonfire, and Kernik, the Prince of Conjurors, was its scalding center.

Kernik called out a word or name that no one knew. The horses trotted backwards, then stood on their hind limbs and seemed to freeze in that position, like statues.

The riders separated from each other and some came forward. Suddenly the street was full of tumblers and music and the beat of tabors, and in the middle, unchained, a bear dancing sedately. And the fur of the bear was blond, and its eyes were blue.

The villagers were over their alarm. The rhythms and the dancing warmed and excited them, and fear was slipping away. They clustered at the dim perimeter of the wide street, and chuckled and applauded and shouted out in surprise. Not very often, they told each other, did you see a show like this.

Now there was a young girl dancing with the bear, and she wore a net of sapphires over her bright yellow hair. The bear was very courteous to her, holding her meekly by the waist and hand, and bowing to her in the manner of the dance. She was so lovely the youths of the village did not even dig each other in the ribs or whistle, though their eyes were round and their faces flushed.

"Behold beauty and innocence. She is a princess and her blood is purer than pearls. Even the bear will not harm her," Kernik's voice recited to the tempo of the drums. "If you will, I shall show you what befell the fair one."

What happened next was hard to explain, though it seemed quite reasonable at the time. The piece of the village where Kernik and his actors stood ceased to be an earth road, all goat-dung and pebbles, and became a landscape of marble with slender trees from whose branches hung golden apples, and under whose latticed shadows drifted birds with tails of green and blue fire. And here the fair girl walked, gathering dazzling fruit in an apron of jewels, while the bear walked after, playing a pipe most tunefully.

"A tranquil scene," crooned the voice of Kernik, "but not for long. There was, in those parts, a dragon."

Overhead thunder rolled. It seemed to fill the sky and burst it. Women screamed.

"Are you afraid to see the dragon come?" roared Kernik. "Speak, and I will turn him back."

"No!" shouted the crowd in delighted fright, "Show us the dragon."

Kernik then again called the secret word, and the dragon came. The sky went red, the sky went blank white. Out of the white, like a lightning bolt, came a beast in a chain-mail of diamonds. Fireworks exploded from its mouth and its tongue was a serpent as long as a hoe. Back shrank the crowd. The bear fled and the birds vanished. The dragon lashed its tail like a huge cat, and struck flame from the roof of a nearby home: yet the roof did not fall and the awful dragon breath scorched no one. It had eyes only for the princess. It seized her in its claws, then straight up like a rocket it went to the highest peak of the marble land and laid her down there and glared about it, flapping its bat's wings.

"Now, who will rescue the lovely one from the foul one?" asked the voice of Kernik. "Come, any offers?"

As if in answer, a buffoon arrived on the marble plain, very fat, with a wooden sword at his side, riding a blue goat with two heads.

"Giddy up!" blustered the buffoon, "I must save the princess!"

The blue goat stopped still and the buffoon got off. The goat butted him and the buffoon fell over. When he tried to remount, the goat shied suddenly and down he went again. One of the goat's heads began to whistle and the other to sing in perfect harmony with it; meanwhile it stood on three legs and made water. When it saw the dragon, it was abruptly. The singing head saw first and fell quiet. The whistling head, puzzled, looked about till it saw the dragon as well. At this, it relinquished its third activity and fled sideways out of sight.

"Oh dragon!" stupidly bellowed the buffoon, "Where are you? Come out and fight. I will make mincemeat of you and a quilt of your skin."

Then he, too, saw the dragon. The dragon flapped its wings. The buffoon tried to run to safety and fell over his sword three times before he managed it.

The crowd, laughing, hissed and disparaged him, and the dragon lashed its tail.

"This is no use," said the voice of Kernik. "Up there is a princess waiting to be rescued. Up there is a dragon waiting to be fought. Surely somewhere there is a champion worthy of both."

The crowd responsively began to cry, "A champion! A champion!" And after a moment a figure strode onto the stage and flung back his black cloak. The crowd gave a cheer, for there was no mistaking the champion had come.

His armor was gold and his helm gold with a silver crest, and in his hand a green-gold sword. His hair and brows were very dark, his features noble, aquiline and arresting. The girls of the village fell silent and held their breath.

The dragon opened its wings and the champion looked up at it without a trace of fear.

"Come down," suggested the champion courteously, in his arrestingly musical voice. "I have something for you, dragon. My sword blade."

The dragon gave a shriek of anger which resembled all the rusty bellows in the Korkeem going at once, and descended like an avalanche.

Then there was a fight indeed.

The young village men fought it too, shaking their fists, howling advice, ducking and spinning round in circles. The young girls fought the battle in their hearts and lungs, and buried their faces in their hands and looked between their fingers.

First the dragon had the knight down, then the knight had the dragon down. Then the dragon breathed out fire and the knight's cloak seemed to catch alight so he must roll on the ground to put it out, and the dragon slashed him with its great curved claws. Then, to an uproar of drums, the champion knight leaned back against one of the glittering trees as if faint from the dragon's breath, and the dragon sprang, and, as it came, the knight's sword flashed up and impaled it through the breast. Black blood flowed from the wound, the dragon fell over, briefly kicking and trumpeting, then leadenly motionless, a last curl of smoke retreating from its nostril.

The audience stamped and clapped.

A spangled chariot was already coming from the marble peak with the beautiful princess in it. A rain of flowers and sweets began to fall as the smiling girl stepped out and the golden champion kissed her hand.

Then a sound, half-recollected, the snap of the showman's fingers, the clack of his nails, and there was only the flicker of the lamps falling on the wide street, a white collapsing mountain—a cloth from under which tumblers were tumbling—and a dragon of wood and glass gems dividing into three pieces, and disgorging men.

Kernik stepped forward, his hands tucked now into his sombre sleeves. He stretched his crayoned mouth, and nodded, and there stood all his actors in a line, though somehow it was still hard to count them, still difficult to be

sure how many of them there were. Or were not. A mass
of tumblers, dragon-men, heads and legs of the goat. Only
three seemed definite, the fat buffoon with a look to him
yet of a blond bear, and the handsome knight and the gorgeous lady, hand in hand. And when all bowed low, the
shadowy ones did so in shadowy fashion, but the buffoon
extravagantly, the princess sweetly, the knight with a
charming and mercurial grin.

"Have we earned our supper, people?" asked Kernik.
"We will tell fortunes after, and besides, the tricks are not
all done."

The villagers bawled their assent. They might have been
drinking white wine.

Mikli and his sons ran to open the doors of their barn,
and wives scattered to bring kindling, cauldrons, supper,
even to kill chickens for the pot, as if poverty, and tomorrow's empty plate meant nothing to them.

Old Ash's wife was hurrying towards the house, and
Shaina shrank aside.

"Slave! Slave!" cried the woman. The dog barked furi-
ously, and scratched his fleas.

'We are all bewitched,' thought Shaina, and icy flames
ran down her spine.

Mikli's barn had not been thrown open in this way since
the wedding of his eldest son three years before. Now
some of the things in it were tossed out on the street, and
the things left inside were sat on. Beer came in skins, food
in pans, and a great hearth was made on the stone floor
and a great fire got going inside it. No one questioned. No
one held back. Items came out of cupboards and off hooks
that had been set by since last winter, and nothing was
grudged.

Kernik, the Clever Showman, sat enthroned on a bale of
hay, shining purple and saffron, and smiled like a kind father as the people brought him their offerings. To his left
sat the maiden in her sapphires, to his right the black-
haired actor who had been the knight, but near or far in a
riot dashed the other players of the troupe.

Sometimes the tumblers turned cartwheels or ran
through hoops or leaped over the fire or danced in it.
Sometimes the bear-buffoon rose and joined them, and
juggled and drew silver eggs from ears and snakes from
out of aghast mouths.

It was the actress-princess who told fortunes. She
stretched out her pale hands and caught between them
the scared hands of girls and wives and grannies, and the
hot hands of the young men who wanted only to touch
her. She told them things from their past that were true,
and things from their future which they believed. No one
dared kiss or grab her cool flesh, nor stare too long into
her regal eyes that were like pools of darkness. Some of
the girls were bolder with the young actor. They slid into
his arms and set their lips to his face and curling hair, and
rubbed against him like cats after cream. He laughed with
them, he paid them compliments and kissed the pretty
ones back, but there was no depth to these courtesies, they
were like shadows thrown on the walls. The village girls
grew uneasy presently, and slunk away.

Shaina at first was pushed to the middle of the barn, to
tend the fire and the pots left on it, and to take drink to
the men when they yelled. But later, when it would be
easy to slip away, she meant to, and bit by bit was edging
to the door in readiness. She wanted to run back up the
street to Old Ash's house. Part of her wanted to hide under her ragged blanket there. She had, from the beginning,
sensed a smell of perversity on the air as surely as a fox
scents dogs. And yet, when later came, she did not quite
go, could not quite make herself leave the barn and run to
the safe house. And now she was growing sleepy, crouched
there in the smoke at the door.

Was all the gold real gold? And the golden armor and
the golden sword, and the gold the firelight found somehow on the black curls of the young actor's hair? Twice
she had passed him, carrying beer to Old Ash, or to stupid
Mikli. The young actor's eyes caught the lamps in blue-
green stars when he raised them, but he did not seem to
see her go by. A blade grazed her then, a blade of iron not
gold. Silly Shaina, slave in a peasant's house, foolish even
to think of him, and he a free man, and better than any of
them. . . . But the dragon had seemed alive and terrible,
how could that be? Kernik—Magic-Maker, Stealer of
Scenes—with, seated on his right hand his chief player,
like the dark young god the maidens worshipped in
spring. . . .

In the night, the dogs were howling again. Perhaps there
were wolves after all, as Old Ash had said, late wolves, or
the kind that were really devils.

Shaina discovered she had fallen asleep. A dream came by. The dream had the actor's face and his voice, but he did not speak to her and his eyes did not answer hers.

Wan light stole over her eyelids, cool as water. The smells of wood-ash and old food were familiar enough, but not the smell of the hay and the cattle and the other ripe reek of beer.

Shaina woke and found herself lying at the door of the barn. All around others snored and grunted in heavy slumber.

Something was the matter with the world this day.

She moved only a little, just enough to see outside.

It was the melancholy grey time immediately before dawn. Sad birds were singing from the slim trees on the mountain slopes, and from the willows by the stream. The houses of the village humped ominous and silent. Seven or nine or thirteen black horses stood waiting like a funeral, and on their backs seven or nine or thirteen riders in black cloaks.

Shaina, her eyes wide, conscious vaguely of witnessing what she was not meant to witness, looked in vain for a bear-buffoon, jugglers, acrobats, looked in vain for a fair-haired girl, a handsome actor. Each rider now was anonymous as each, and all their color, their panache, their brazen brightness was gone. The jewels then were maybe glass, after all, and the Showman only a trickster travelling to a fair at Kost.

Then the first sun-ray struck over the mountain, the sky was lit, and as the uncountable troupe began to pass along the street, Shaina saw something was missing from them, something was left out. They so resembled shadows, man, girl or beast, but not one *cast* a shadow on the road.

Her instincts leapt. She wanted to make holy signs to protect herself, to spit the nearness of evil and unlife out of her mouth. But all she could think was: 'He also, the young actor, is a demon. He also.'

And then she remembered how he had looked at her and not seen her, looked and not seen with those eyes the color of sea water and smoke. And so it was from a memory that the sword went through her, but through her the sword went, straight through her heart, as Barbayat, the Grey Lady, had cruelly promised.

☀ **3** ☀

Shaina went to the well. She looked into it. But the well was a poor mirror, like all the rest.

She did not understand what to do; she did not understand herself. All the amorphous pain that had welled up in her before, all that longing without a name, had now found a name, and with a name it was no better.

Love was like a wild beast gnawing her heart and her vitals. She had been too proud and too outcast and too self-sufficient to know it before. Men had come and gone in the village, some of them not so bad, some of them strong and good-looking, and maybe some of them had looked at her thoughtfully, even though she was Old Ash's slave. But this was where the ghosts in her took charge, the race memories, the ancestor voices of her forgotten land. They made her see brutishness in place of strength, and alienness in every male gesture, and nothing in her had ever stirred. She had been impervious and like all impervious things, it had taken, at the correct moment, only one look, one dream, to break in the bolted door.

Presently, sweeping the yard vigorously, she begged her own pardon and told herself that it was not her fault after all, the witch of Cold Crag had put a curse on her.

There were indeed plenty of curses that strange morning.

Shaina, in her preoccupation, did not grasp immediately what was wrong in the village. She had set about her tasks as usual, throwing herself into back-breaking work rather as someone would bite his cheek with the toothache, trying to offset one pain with another. There was sweeping and fetching water, lighting the first fire of day with the words properly spoken over it—although generally Old Ash's wife superintended this—the feeding of chickens, probably the milking of goats if Young Ash was indisposed. Once or twice, though not very often, there had been a celebration in Mikli's barn before, but the morning after, work

24

went on much as ever, the men trudging off to the fields
with their sore heads, the women grumbling back to their
houses. But today everyone seemed late in coming, and the
sun was well up before there was any activity other than
Shaina's own and the growling of the dogs. Also, when a
sound did come it was a loud sound, a raucous complaint,
and from more than one throat.

Along the crooked street surged men and women,
shouting. The dogs began to bark, cows heavy with milk
mooed like a discontented orchestra, and birds rushed into
the sky to get away from it all.

Mikli was waving his fists and his sons were offering to
fight whoever cared to. Someone's brother from Kost was
saying somebody would shortly land in prison. A woman
was screeching that she had been taken against her will,
and an old man quavering that 'they' had stolen his chickens, while several voices were declaring that chickens
might run in a circle but whoever had stolen their beer
skins would be hearing about it.

Nevertheless, the inbred, instinctual laws of land and
hearth were proving too strong, and even as the crowd still
threatened and accused, it was breaking up into its separate dwellings, running off towards the cowpens or pick-
ing up farm implements. Old Ash came thundering into
the yard, grabbed a hunk of bread and went off with it to
fetch the plough. The wife came after and cast only one
sharp look at Shaina.

"You're up early, slave. Did you hear anyone stealing
chickens in the night? Or beer?"

"I beg your pardon, no, I did not," said Shaina politely.

"Useless wretch that you are," snapped the wife, and
clipped her, as usual, round the ear. "Get off and see to
the goats, and then take them up the mountain. Young
Ash is singing his old song. What I have done to offend
the gods I can't tell, that they should give me a sot for a
son and a clod for a slave. Be off, I said. You don't need a
breakfast, you're too plump as it is. One should be able to
number the bones of a slave and I'm sure I can't number
yours."

Shaina did as she was told. She had learned as early as
seven years that it was best to do so. Yet she was puzzled.
And as she passed through the village, her puzzlement in-
creased.

It seemed that none of them remembered what had happened the night before, the purple showman, Kernik, Prince of Conjurors, the scintillating actors, the wild extravagance of the feast which followed. Oh no, there had been nothing like that. Thieves had got in and taken their chickens and their loaves and their drink, and then locked the villagers in the barn, presumably cook-pots, chicken bones and all—at any rate this was the story they were piecing together for themselves in anger and bewilderment. Only Shaina recalled, and Shaina sensibly kept quiet. She had noticed that, while they did not seem to comprehend, in their confused belligerence, that they had become voluntarily very drunk in the night, their bodies comprehended, and reacted accordingly.

She saw to the milking, and, soon as she could, drove the goat herd out of its pen and up the track towards the mountain. The hubbub she left behind had disconcerted her, and for a while her mind was preoccupied with thoughts and questions. Then abruptly, the air was thin and fragrant about her; she looked back and saw the valley growing small, and it grew small in her mind as well.

Old Ash's wife had neglected to give her the washing and mending basket. Shaina felt a sudden terror. If she sat idle on the mountain, the witch's spell—for what else was it?—would invade her again, and she would see his eyes in the sky and in the green stones, and hear his voice, speaking, laughing, but not to her or with her.

"Goats," said Shaina, "how easy it is to be a goat, did you guess?" What did a goat do when it loved? Why, that was simple. Crude and uncomplex goat, not forced to feel the sword pierce through your goat-heart.

Then she was thinking of the magician, and she found it difficult to do so, as if a wall of mist had formed in her brain between the present and the past. The sorcery he had made was beginning to affect her too, just as it had the others—yet, why did she alone remember anything? She realized now, fully, how strong the magic of Kernik, Prince of Conjurors, must be. Strong and awesome, to sweep away the memory of a whole night of wonders as a broom sweeps away the trace of birds' feet in the snow. Truly he was a person to be respected and feared, and it would be safe and intelligent to forget entirely his magnificent coming and that sly going that she had not been

meant to see. But of course she could not, and ac-
knowledged simultaneously why she could not.

The young actor rode by the magician.

Perhaps the young actor was bound in service to the
magician, even belonged to him, was a slave, as Shaina
herself was a slave. Shaina began to argue with Shaina.

"Silly girl, he does not cast a shadow."

"So, he does not. Is it his fault? If he is the magician's
slave he has no choice about what he will do in the matter
of shadows. Have I a choice if Old Ash tells me to get
wood?"

"Wood and shadows are not the same."

But Shaina felt a deep wounding tenderness for him,
that he went shadowless; she wanted to find the shadow,
give it back to him—a gift—she wanted—

And there was the pasture, though she had barely noticed coming up the track, and the goats were spreading
out on it, honey-brown and bleating stridently. And there
were the mountains all about, like cut gems in the sunlight, Elf Roof, Black Top. And Cold Crag. And Cold
Crag was quite close, surely only a morning's journey. . . .

"No, Grey Woman," said Shaina aloud, "I won't go
to you."

But she looked down, where a little stream went by
through the goat-nibbled turf, and she saw his face in the
stream as clearly as she had never seen her own. When she
looked up she saw the sky all empty of cloud, like lone-
liness. And when she called to the goats: "Mind the steep
place," or "Eat up the grass nicely," her words echoed
back to her and it seemed she had said: "Love, love, love
is devouring me."

Finally she recalled she had not greeted the rock idol on
the way, which was indisputably a disaster.

"Well then, I am lost," Shaina said philosophically. "I
shall have to visit Cold Crag after all."

Certainly she had no business to go, to leave the goats.
But the goats were busy and happy, and would be quite
safe. What about wolves? No, no, there were no wolves up
here. What about robbers? What about a beating if she lost
any of the herd, or was late back? Oh, that was in the
evening, a whole year of a day away.

Shaina began to walk very fast over the mountain side
and westwards towards the delicate, gloomily-shining fang
of the witch's mountain.

Barbayat, the Grey Lady, lived on the mountain's side, though not consistantly, and it was well known that some people who went looking for her did not find her, while others who would rather have kept out of her way, stumbled on her door by accident.

Cold Crag had earned its name. Black pine trees clung on its flanks, and fogs strolled around it day and night and the sun did not seem to care to call. Sprites lived in caves and crows sat on branches, and it was a steep climb.

When Shaina reached the natural bridge of rock which joined the uplands of the goat pasture to the neighboring heights, it was far later than she had anticipated. And when she had got on to the Crag she must go more slowly still, for the tracks were seldom used and treacherous. She seemed to toil upwards for a month, snatching at the tough stems of the black trees to aid herself, under the sideways eyes of the crows. Then it got so dark and shivered so chill, she half believed that night was coming on. Shaina began to feel angry. She stopped moving and called out:

"If the Grey Lady is anywhere about I hope it's not far, for I'm thinking of turning back."

Immediately about six crows burst out of various trees and clattered away, and when Shaina, who had turned to stare after them, glanced down again, she noticed a bald clearing in the pines that somehow she had not been aware of before. And there, at the edge of the clearing, was a grey stone house like a squat mossy boulder with one twisted chimney from which a snake of smoke was wriggling.

Shaina had the feeling of a frog jumping under her ribs, but she lifted her head higher than the Duke of Arkev's daughter, and she marched across the open place, right up to Barbayat's door.

A round door it was, round as a wheel, and when Shaina knocked on it fiercely it rolled sideways instead of inwards, and there was a witch's room if ever anyone saw one.

Black wooden pillars upheld a domed roof reminiscent of a beehive, and every pillar was carved like a different tall, thin, grim, black person with skinny hands and a hooked or pointed nose. Some of these persons had beards and some had long moustaches, some wore tall hats and some wore flat ones, and several wore cloaks, but this did not hide the fact that several had tails. There were no windows in the stone room, but light came from a tasteful arrangement of seven human skulls hung from the ceiling on an iron chain with candles burning in them. There was also a low fire buzzing on an open hearth. In its sombre red glare, less bright yet more widespread and descriptive than the glow of the skull lamps, unknown objects winked on the walls—bone things, metal things—and symbols drawn there in yellow and white clay seemed to dart, disintegrate and reassemble.

On the east side of the hearth sat a russet fox with garnets for eyes. On the west side was a rocking chair of pale birchwood, and rocking in it, leisurely, prosaically, a shape like a grey boulder.

Shaina's mouth was dry as a drought, but she took a breath and announced:

"The Grey Lady told me someone's look would go through me like a sword, and through me like a sword someone's look has gone. The Grey Lady said I would come begging for her help, and for her help I have come, though whether I shall beg is another matter. I trust the Grey Lady is both pleased and satisfied."

The boulder spoke:

" 'Don't you just admire my new necklace', said the chained dog."

"Pardon me," said Shaina quickly, "it's not like that."

"Is it not?"

"Indeed no."

"Well then, take your chain and go away, slave-maiden, for I can see quite well how you are tied to the post."

Shaina hesitated, then she said:

"Very well. I beg you to help me."

"How do you know that I can?" asked the boulder, shifting a little now so that one piercing eye flashed in the firelight.

"As you mentioned, they know of you in the village. Some say your charms work, others say they don't."

"A mere charm will not do for you," said Barbayat, "you'll need stronger medicine than that."

"Yes," said Shaina, and abruptly tears welled in her throat, but she pushed them down, though the words that spilled out were like the tears, desolate and aching and bright. "He came and he went, and there will be mountains between us now—but he casts no shadow—"

"That I know," said Barbayat impatiently. "Do you think all this clutter here is for nothing? I have a certain crystal, I looked in it. I saw Volkhavaar who calls himself Kernik, he of the purple and the nails, and with his pretty dragon, too. Oh, you are in deep and near drowning. All who ride with Volkhavaar are his, and your young man is his too, even with his black so-curling hair and his sea-smoke eyes—skpah! Better go to the wolf and say 'Eat me' or to the bear and say 'Hug me', than love him."

"Mother," said Shaina, "you told me I would come to you, and presumably you saw an advantage for yourself in so doing or you would not have troubled. Now, why are you trying to put cold in my heart, and water in my bones?"

"Because," said Barbayat, turning all the way around now towards Shaina, "it will only make you want him more when I tell you how dangerous it is to want, and how unlikely it is that you will succeed in obtaining more than your death."

"I don't need to be told that," said Shaina, seating herself wearily on the witch's hard floor. "After all, he is gone, and how can a slave follow? I am not free to leave the village, if I went they would say I had run, and set the dogs after me. Once a man stole a pig and they chased him with dogs. He did not come back, only his boots with blood on them. The dogs catch everything their masters let them catch. They would catch me."

"You will have worse than dogs after you, slave-maiden, that much is in your stars for sure. But I will say this: men may enslave bodies. But not what lives in them."

Silence then. The fox scratched, the fire licked itself. Shaina bowed her head on her knees. She felt exhausted, and tremendously, luxuriously sad, like a child ready to cry itself to sleep. Yet at the same instant her skin prickled, for she knew Barbayat was about to tell her a magic that would alter everything.

"What lives in bodies, Barbayat?" Shaina murmured at last, pronouncing the witch's name, even though she knew it was reckoned unwise to do so.

"*Souls,*" said Barbayat. "Listen. I will make it plain. Then I will tell you what I want from you, and then we will strike a bargain, or we will not strike one, as the case may be."

Shaina nodded. The floor felt quite soft to her now, and

the fox had come near and was gazing in her face with its blazing eyes, so intently that it dazzled her and her own lids fell shut.

"Everything has a soul," said Barbayat, but her voice had merged with and become the sonorous crackle of the fire. "The land has a soul, and every tree and mountain, every lake and flower, and every bird, fish and beast that is in it. This is the substance from which all our pleasures and sorrows are built. Love and hate and even sorcery spring from the soul.

"Now this is the manner of it. While on earth, the soul resembles the body, for the body is the clay in which it is cast, and the cloak which it must wear. Beyond earth the soul is changed, and I shall not be telling you how, neither would you understand me. While your body lives, however, your soul may still leave it and have adventures on its own. If so, your soul will have these properties: it will be as you are, but pale and transparent in appearance, very like those creatures men call ghosts. It will need neither food nor drink nor breath, and nothing mortal can harm it—stick, stone, iron; tooth of hound nor claw of eagle, nor flame nor water, neither falling from any height, for the soul flies without wings, swifter than a bird, in time or out of it, and needs no rest. As you can see, it can do well enough without the heavy flesh that restrains it. But set free your Soul, and you will notice the shining cord that joins it still to your body as the birth-cord joins the infant to the mother. Fine as a strand of silk is the cord that binds the soul, in color silver, yet stronger than the strongest. Go where you will, it will stretch as far as it must; it will not hold you back, neither will it tear or break. Only death snaps that chain, but Lord Death is always close with his net.

"The soul may be independent of the flesh, but the flesh without the soul is helpless as snail without shell. Look, and you will see your body lying as if in a deep slumber, but look *closely*; you will find no breathing. Now I will tell you something you must remember whatever else you forget. For a short span only may the soul desert the body. The later you are from home, the worse for your house it will be. The first night—say, to reckon it, midnight to the rise of the sun—the body will do well enough. Be back at dawn, no harm is done. But be absent after that and there will be a change. The tides will slacken in the veins, the brain grows sluggish and the organs begin to fail. Return then, you will be sick for a year of months. But do not return, and presently the appearance of the body will not inspire confidence. People in the place will call a physician or the priest, and soon there will be *no* returning. The ground it will be then, and a black hole dug in it. And once the body is in the grave, the soul alone cannot linger for long. Pale winds blow it out of this world into another one. Goodbye then earth's pain and winter, greenness and joy, and farewell to loving and beloved."

Somewhere sparks sizzled in the fire, or in Barbayat's voice.

"But if you take care, and you desire it, Shaina-slave, while your body sleeps, or seems to, in the peasant's dwelling, your silver soul may be seeking its heart's love over the mountains, swifter than a bird. Soul calls to soul, and soul answers. When you find him, can you doubt his soul will wake to the yearning in yours? How can he fail to love you also? Love does not come as your love came unless there is already a bond between the two of you, and, if he is blind to it now, his spirit will see with different eyes. So, maiden, Barbayat knows how the soul may be freed. But you will need seven days teaching, and seven days payment I will ask for it."

The fox licked Shaina's face.

She started, her eyes opened; she caught her breath and her heart hammered. She had heard every syllable, she could have recited Barbayat's words back to her.

"If I am—insubstantial, not flesh—how shall I find the way to him?" Shaina whispered.

"Soul calls soul, I said. You love him. You will know the way though twenty mountains and ten seas stand between you."

"What payment then?"

" 'What payment then?' Yes, yes," said Barbayat. Her black glance was again like two knives. "When I tell you that, you may jump up and run away. But recollect this, I might have taken it while you were drowsing there from my pretty's fox's look, and not awakened you and struck bargains."

Shaina got to her feet and clenched her hands. Her eyes, chestnut-colored, almost copper in the fire-gloom, were wide and full of hunger, but her mouth was set.

"What then? Tell me now."

"Seven days you come to me. Seven things I teach you. Seven times you give me your wrist and I drink from the vein there."

"My blood!" exclaimed Shaina. "*Oh*, no."

"Please yourself," said Barbayat the witch, the boulder, the vampire, rocking in her birchwood chair.

"Why?" demanded Shaina, her face white, trembling.

"To live," said Barbayat resolutely. "That is how I have cheated Lord Death so long. When he comes with his net, knocking on his round door at midnight, 'Wait, sir,' I say, and I find a maiden, a virgin, one in need of a charm or a lesson, and I charge my fee. Only maiden's blood will do me good. I don't take much, she doesn't die of it, and I live. Life is good. Perhaps someone else thinks so too."

There came a whirling in Shaina's head. All at once she saw a young man bound on a wheel of iron; his hair was black, his white body marbled with purple wounds, and his face forever empty.

"No!" Shaina cried.

"Yes. Volkhavaar the Cruel has taken a new road and many will perish on the way. Your sweetheart also, perhaps, unless you save him."

"You make illusions, as the magician did, to trick me."

"Leave then," said Barbayat, "learn nothing, let him go and maybe find a girl elsewhere or a grave elsewhere. Tell yourself your dreams are illusion. You will never be sure. Better be content with stale beer in comfort than drink white wine with danger."

Shaina looked about. She saw the fox. The fox seemed to say to her: 'When I was younger and ran free in the forest, a hunter caught my mate and stunned him with a blow and locked him in a cage. I went to the place in the broad white of the spring moon; near to the hunter's fire I went, near enough to hear his man's breathing and see the flamelight catch on the knife in his hand. I gnawed through the bars of the cage and dragged at my mate, and half carried him as I would carry a cub, away into the trees. My paws were sore, I lost a tooth, my back pained me and I was afraid, but I never thought I could do otherwise. That is what love is.'

Shaina looked away. She saw her own hands knotted together. She thought: 'If I must choose, then I have chosen.' She said to the witch: "Yes," and formally, "will you drink now?"

Barbayat laughed. It was not exactly like a woman's laughter.

"It's late," she said. "One day makes little odds for either you or me. Go home and come tomorrow."

Shaina went to the door. Time had gone fast. Between the pines two black crows were circling over the low red disc of the sun. Indeed it was late. She would not get home before moonrise, worse than yesterday. And definitely she would be beaten.

"The rod strikes the back, not the heart," said Shaina to the witch, and somehow she found herself smiling. "I will come tomorrow." But supposing, she added in her mind, Young Ash does not get drunk and brings the goats to the mountain himself? Shaina, she thought, don't be a fool. It's your business to make sure that he *does* get drunk.

Then she began to run—out of the door, down the slope of Cold Crag, the black trees rattling by, down and down to the rocky bridge, across it, and down again, and over the uplands, to the goat-grazing. She went faster going down than she had climbing up, yet not fast enough. The sun's chariot had sunk from view and the sky was all golden afterglow deepening swiftly into violet when she burst into the pasture.

A sudden anxiety for the herd had made her run more quickly on the last lap, but every goat seemed to be there, each standing rather close to its neighbors, nibbling, bleating and butting heads in a friendly way. They all turned and looked at her, and told each other: "Here is Shaina, out of breath."

She was glad to see them.

Dizzy from the descent and the strange day, dizzy from everything that had happened, she crossed the turf and began to make the homeward gestures and noises to them. At that moment four crows rose from the four quarters of the field, up into the fading gold roof of the sky. Perhaps they had only been searching out grubs, but it might be that the Grey Lady had sent them to guard the herd in Shaina's place. Somehow, vampire or not, Shaina trusted Barbayat.

"I am happy, I think," the slave said to her master's goats. Her heart no longer hurt, it flamed. She was troubled to find herself so joyous in the face of such dark tomorrows, weird bargains, terrible uncertainties.

The stick rose and fell on Shaina's back that night, but Old Ash was not unduly harsh—at least, for the owner of a slave he was not. He did not want to harm her since he could not afford to buy another in her place.

"Wretch of a girl," said Old Ash's wife. "I am surprised she did not run off with the thieves yesterday, the good-for-nothing, thankless slut." Clearly she was itching to get hold of the stick herself, but Old Ash did not let her. Shaina bore the punishment, as ever, without flinching and without a cry. Presently the rain of blows ceased and her mind was able to get to work on other matters.

After the meal, she took the scraps into the yard and fed the dog, and saw Young Ash slouched moodily by the wall, his underlip thrust out.

Overhead the moon burned pure and white. The mountains seemed made of silver, and their shadows of ebony, and Lady Spring herself was in the air, sweet as pinewood and sharp as a knife.

Shaina set out the food for the dog, which snarled and showed, without gratitude, its slim brown fangs. Hearing the clatter of the dish, Young Ash muttered nastily:

"Does your back sting, slave? Does it throb? I hope it does."

"Yes, by your leave," said Shaina.

"Good. I'm glad I'm not the only one to be suffering tonight, you from the rod and me from my dry throat. By my boots, if I don't get a drink, I shall be shrivelled up by morning."

"But the inn is only over the hill," said Shaina.

"She says I must stay home, the old witch, Mother Earth pardon me. She says she is tired of my drinking. As if I can help it if the thieves forced liquor down my throat last night. Is that my fault? Have you ever known me drunk otherwise?"

"Indeed *not*," replied Shaina, outraged. "It's understood from here to Kost, that Young Ash can outdrink any man born and still remain sober as salt."

Young Ash hitched up his belt, gratified.

"Just what I have always said."

"One day," said Shaina, artfully, slipping closer, "Young Ash will be master of the house. Then his mother may wish she had been more circumspect. When she is a poor old widow and relies on your strong arms for her bread, she will not dare say: 'Go here, stay there.' "

"Quite right. Quite right: What a smart minx you are. Well then, I'll be away at once, and confound her." Young Ash began to whistle his walking-to-the-tavern tune, then broke off. "If she asks where I am——"

"Why," said Shaina demurely, "aren't you helping mend Gula's plough?"

"So I am." Young Ash slapped his thigh, gave Shaina a violent, almost brotherly kiss, and hurried off up the crooked street under the watching moon.

Shaina, Shaina, said the stars up in the black night sky, what are you doing? Are you sharpening your wits on the stones?

Shaina, Shaina, said Old Ash's wife whirling spinning wheel, why do the thoughts go round in your head like me?

Shaina, Shaina, sighed the rug on which she later lay by the fire, go to sleep and be ready for tomorrow.

Shaina, said the dawn under the door, wake up! Here comes Young Ash with beer in his belly as high as his eyes, and here comes the day walking over the mountain, the day when the witch buys your maiden's blood with her spell.

Shaina, said her heart, hurry! Hurry!

✳ 4 ✳

What shouts, imprecations, fury: Old Ash's wife. Young Ash sprawled, holding his head: never again. *Indeed* not.

Shaina ran with the goats, ran up the mountain. Shaina ran higher, over the rocky bridge. The goats watched her go, and laughed and nodded tolerantly. Up the cold slope of the witch's mountain toiled Shaina, still half running.

And there was the grey house with the twisted chimney, and Shaina hardly knew how she got to it so fast.

Then by the round door, her heart in her throat knocking, urging her hand to knock too. Shaina knocked, but she felt icy now from heel to crown. The door opened, sideways, as before, and the room was in front of her, as before. Yet not quite.

On the ground was drawn a magic shape in white clay.

Shaina hesitated when she saw that shape, but out of the red fire-gloom between the skinny black pillar-people came the stony little voice of Barbayat.

"Come in. Fear nothing. Think of him with his curling hair."

Shaina stepped over the threshold.

The skull lamps were not lit today. An iron bowl stood on an iron tripod in the middle of the magic drawing on the floor, and from the bowl rose a flowery-smelling smoke, and next to the tripod was a stool.

The fox, not Barbayat, was rocking in the birchwood chair. Shaina looked about, and then over her shoulder, and sure enough there Barbayat was, in the one place she could not possibly be, exactly behind in the doorway.

"Are you thinking of him? Of his hair and his eyes and his fine young man's body? Doesn't it make you feel better? Go and sit. Yes, there where the stool is set for you."

Shaina crossed over the white clay with a tingling in her arteries, and sat as the witch had told her to.

"Surely not scared?" asked Barbayat.

"Humbly, yes," said Shaina.

37

"Then perhaps you've changed your mind?"

"I have not."

Into the clay drawing came Barbayat, and sat down at Shaina's feet.

"Let me have your wrist."

Shaina started.

"Am I to pay the gold before I see the pig?"

"So you are. I will tell you something. This is not all one-sided business. When some of your bright blood flows in my grey veins, I will understand you better, and the better I understand you the better able shall I be to teach you what you must know." Barbayat paused, just like a boulder on the floor. "Shall I tell you his name?"

"Whose name?"

"His, the young actor's name. Who else's would you be interested in?"

"How do you know it?"

"I have a clever crystal. Names are easy to discover. Other things harder. Well?"

"Yes. Tell me, of course, tell me."

"His name is Dasyel," said the witch, took Shaina's wrist and bit it.

Shaina felt nothing. The curious enchantment of learning how he was to be called had worked its own spell. Yet the smoke in the iron bowl was dissolving her thoughts, and the room was floating away, up over Cold Crag, and she with it. Dasyel, her mind whispered to her, half asleep, the painless mouth sipping so gently, gently. She began to imagine that the little grey witch was her child at her breast; perhaps, too, his child, something loved and vulnerable, seeking nourishment, which she gave gladly and without regret. . . . She had an urge to stroke Barbayat's mossy head.

"Wake up, daughter," said a voice, and Shaina obeyed, and found the fox had pressed its cool damp nose to her neck.

"Did you speak?" Shaina asked the fox. It yawned and sat down beside her. There was no longer a white clay shape on the floor.

"Do you suppose you can hear the language of beasts now?" inquired Barbayat, in a contemptuous yet kindly tone. "It was I who spoke to you, Shaina of the midnight hair. It is the hour that is neighbor to sunset, but if you go quick, you will be back before dark."

Shaina stretched. She felt a little giddy, yet not unwell. About her left wrist was tied a piece of clean bleached linen.

"But, Barbayat, have you told me anything?"

"Think, silly child. There, do you see the knowledge in your brain? I taught you while you slept so you would not forget it. In the low dark hours after midnight, you must practice all I have said."

Shaina touched her brow, surprised at all the strange images that were now trying to crowd it—the spells and disciplines the witch had given her, in exchange for her salty drink.

"Stand up now, daughter," said Barbayat. "You will do well enough. Keep the linen in place, and if any ask, say you scratched yourself on a flint or a bramble. On no account let the priest see it or we shall all have troubles. You won't miss what I took. Come again tomorrow."

Shaina went to the door, then glanced back. She glanced at Barbayat rocking in her chair, and Barbayat had a different look to her, hard to define. Was she a little straighter, a little pinker? Were her eyes, though just as sharp, a little nearer warmth?

"Yes, I am looking well, am I not," said the witch. "Not all wine is good, and of the good, some is better than the rest."

"I will do what you taught me," said Shaina, "and come tomorrow, only—"

"Only what?"

"Young Ash may not get drunk tonight—and then there are five nights more."

Barbayat nodded.

"In your mind I left something besides the rest. Can you see it?"

"Why," said Shaina, half laughing, "what a spell indeed! That will prove useful."

Outside the sky was reddening behind the pines. Shaina fled down Cold Crag and back to the goats, and this time was not amazed to see four black crows up into the air at her approach.

No beating that night. She was home in time.

So first, the magic lighting of the evening fire, next, the serving of supper, the clearing of plates, and eventually, Old Ash's wife's spinning wheel turning in the corner. Old

Ash snoozed by the hearth, Young Ash went to the water
pitcher, for after last night's beer-drinking, he was still
thirsty. He dipped in his mug, and Shaina whispered, far
down under her breath:

"Water, you are not what you think. Water, you did not
come out of the cool earth, you came from a stock with
the sun on it; you got picked and trampled and stored in a
jar. Water, do you know what you are? Water, you are a
sweet white wine."

Young Ash drank, and drank again, and Shaina knew
that in the night he would drink maybe twice more.

"Water, you are very strong wine, but slow. Don't go
fast. Don't show what you are till morning."

"What's the wretch muttering?" demanded the wife,
glaring from her spinning. "Putting a curse on us all, I
shouldn't wonder. Watch yourself, slave, I'll have the stick
to you."

In the night the moon drifted low as a sinking ship. The
wind sighed. "Dasyel," said the wind. "I hear you," said
Shaina, and hugged her own self for love of him.

Then she spoke the words the witch had told her, the
words that ultimately would free her soul. And she made
the charm, using her voice, her hands, her brain. Presently
she felt a sharp pain between her eyes, first cold, then hot,
as the witch had said she would.

"He's drunk!" screamed Old Ash's wife in the morning,
"And for the life of me I don't know how he got at
liquor—I'll swear he didn't stir foot nor finger out of
doors since supper."

Off with the goats ran Shaina, up the mountain, over
the rock bridge, along the slope of Cold Crag, and into
Barbayat's house. That day, and five days after.

"Mother, am I ready? Am I wise enough? Shall I be
able to do it?"

"Daughter, yes, you are, you are, and you shall."

"Mother, I feel doubt. Can I find him as you say, simply by loving him?"

"Wait and see. You won't doubt when the time comes.
Already, perhaps, some part of him, your Dasyel, senses
you will follow him. Perhaps others sense it. Perhaps the
Cruel One, Volkhavaar of the Purple Sleeves, perhaps he
senses too, so beware."

"I'm not afraid. Yes, but I am afraid. I shall not mind it. The past five nights I've felt the house demons watching me, watching what I do. I felt their whisperings. They also fear the magician. I will beware."

"Stand up, then. Maybe we shall not meet again."

"Unless the spell fails."

"Possibly, the sun has died in the night," said Barbayat.

Shaina's wrist was bound by a new clean linen, but it was the last. The bargain was completed, or would be when tonight her spirit left her flesh—Oh, was it believable? Yes.

Each day the vampire had milked her. Shaina no longer experienced surprise that, instead of being repulsed by this activity, she had thereby grown oddly closer to the witch, and the witch to her. Their polite interchange of titles— mother, daughter—was no more courtesy. In a way, the orphan slave had been fostered, in a way, the barren witch had created offspring. Shaina now looked into Barbayat's face with intimacy and actual affection. Still a boulder, it was hard to tell what Barbayat precisely thought. Then, all at once, the witch took Shaina's hand, and kissed her on the cheek, like the mother she had become. And when she stepped back, Shaina stared.

There was a great change in Barbayat, though visible only for a moment before the veneer of mossy stone swathed her again. She was taller, straighter; she had a pride of carriage and an elegance of bearing; her skin was creamy and unlined, her eyes bright black-green and clear as a child's, yet with such a store of accumulated powers and strengths in them that they were essentially old for all that. Her hair poured down her back, black as Shaina's own; indeed, she had an appearance of Shaina altogether, Shaina's striking looks, her vitality, her goodness, her iron endurance; if not the innocence that could only exist in a young girl.

"That is *your* magic, maiden," said Barbayat, "That is the spell you worked on *me*. Go now, and try my magic in the dark hours beyond midnight. Run fast or you will be late again."

Then Barbayat was Barbayat once more, the Grey Lady, and the fox barked by the hearth.

Shaina ran down the mountain. She could hardly wait for night.

What with the 'thieves' and the wolves and the mystery

of Young Ash's constant, inexplicable drunkenness, the valley was restless, fires and lamps burned late, and even a priest had been sent for from Kost. The village sensed the supernatural had touched it, but it did not look twice at the slave girl. Yet.

Presently the house snored, and Shaina lay by the ashes of the fire, in the low ebb hours the other side of midnight.

She spoke the charm, she recited the words, she made the gestures and the signs, she emptied her mind, she looked out and upwards, through the rafters and the roof, straight through the smoky demons lying there, up into the black high sky, jewelled with stars.

Heat and cold, snow and fire, fell on her skin. Not only her forehead, but her whole body. She felt a well gape for her, the depth of a great precipice, and knew that to topple forward into it must be to lose herself forever. And part of her cried out to be still, to return, to pull back from this dreadful abyss. But Shaina, breathing, murmuring the ritual, thrust with her spirit as the swimmer thrusts through a turgid cloying water, outwards, outwards. . . .

A dagger pierced her breast and limbs and belly; an axe clove her skull. Red lights burst across her eyes. She was blind and deaf and dumb—she could not scream. She could not breathe, she could not swallow. But she thrust again, laboring, giving birth to the thing within her. And then—

Metamorphosis. Girl into bird, into air, into dream.

She hung, suspended, disbelieving, electric, the color of cool ice in the dark room. Peace, oh, what lovely peace fell on her. No pain, no struggle, no fear, and finally, no uncertainty.

She looked down.

"Oh, Shaina, Shaina," whispered her soul.

There she lay, as if asleep, her own self, as the witch had promised, bound to her by a slender chain of silver. Shaina saw herself for the first time, far better than in a mirror. Shaina loved herself, and knew herself for the first time, with the pure and proper and needful love and the rare knowledge that comes only with objectivity. And, with that knowing and loving remembered the other love.

"Oh—I know, I *do* know—"

And lifting, rising like steam, up, up through the roof, without wings, swifter than a bird, Shaina's soul burned and turned towards the direction of her love, understanding at once where he was and how she might find him.

Though understanding nothing of the dangers, nothing of the agony to come.

PART TWO

PART TWO

The Magician
and His Power

* 5 *

Since there is soot, even in the best chimney, this turn of the wheel brings Volkhavaar, who occasionally called himself Kernik, Prince of Conjurors, that great Master of Illusion, and of Darkness.

In his youth, the skin of Kernik was yellow, for his mother was a foreign woman who came over distant tall mountains with him in her belly.

When he was small he had no name, for no one bothered to give him one, and he was apparently a stupid sluggish child. But he watched everything very carefully, and presently turned it to his own advantage. His mother had brought him forth in a desolate village, just on the Korkeem side of the Peaks, a place where people were used to seeing traders with such coloring, and took no huge notice of them. Nevertheless, they came to find her a striking creature to be living amongst them, with her saffron flesh, her hair so strange a black it was almost dark green, and her eyes another kind of black that was almost red. Shortly, some of the men began to visit her at night, though secretly, for fear of their wives and the priest.

All that went on, Kernik saw from his rag bed near the fire. He was then about seven or eight, but, with his unfocused look, no one supposed he really noticed anything. Soon, however, the men who came and went with the yellow mother found the yellow child dogging them along the slopes. The child, for all his imbecilic stare, made it clear that either they would do as he asked, or he would run to the priest.

There was something slimy and unwholesome about the child that the men noted then for the first time. Even though so tiny, he scared them, and they did as he said. In point of fact, he did not demand anything very much, they were all bizarre, silly things he wanted: "Bring me that rock up there and put it by the door," "Cough three times when you are coming up the track," yet, despite the triviality of the requests, the men did as they were bid, and the child ruled them as with an iron rod.

Things, naturally, could not go on like this for very long. One night a man missed his footing going down from the yellow woman's hovel, and broke his leg. In his pain and confusion, he blurted where he had been, and quickly gave away other names as well. The village women turned on the foreigner like a pack of wolves, and drove her out, child and all.

Kernik and she trudged for many miles down mountain flanks and over a wide valley. They had to cross a river, and the mother paid for the ferry in her usual way. On the other side were rocky hills mantled in forest, and somewhere in this forest bears ate Kernik's mother, though he was left whole. Perhaps, nasty, skinny brat that he was, they did not think him toothsome.

After his orphaning, Kernik kept alive by eating berries and stolen nest eggs, and he became adept at catching lizards or birds, lying in wait for hours if necessary, then springing with the agility of a cat. The little carcasses he ate raw, blood running down his chin, his fingers stuck with scales or feathers. Eventually, he came on a second village, as poor and as isolated as the one in which he had been born.

Halfway up a solitary mountain it was, built of the felled trunks of pine trees, often grey with the mists that sank down from the bald, generally sunless summit above.

Kernik had gotten very wild during his months alone in the forest. He crept near the village, cautious, predatory, like a wolf. Before long two or three girls and an old woman came up the street to fetch water from the well, and saw him. No doubt he frightened them. He looked certainly more beast than human, and ferocious beast too, with his uncanny skin, his matted black hair, his filthy fingernails growing as long or longer than the talons of eagles, and his teeth sharp from the bones of birds. He had forgotten human speech, or nearly, but somehow not his cunning, and somehow, somewhere in his brief oblique career, he had learned the one action that softens the hearts of most women. He crouched down and wept.

The girls, who had been about to run for their husbands and brothers, hesitated. The old woman gave a cry. She was a widow and barren, and she had always longed for a child. Now some good spirit of the forest had seen fit to answer, if somewhat belatedly, the prayers and entreaties of her youth. Here was a little boy—a son. Vile, atrocious, bestial he might be, but in need he was, and she could reply to that need. Her misguided heart warmed and opened, and she took Kernik into her arms and her house.

Kernik's hair was cut, his nails trimmed, his body washed and dressed in homespun. He lived in the old woman's house, and she gave him a name, but he forgot it, and pretty soon, by various insidious means, he had her under his thumb. He was then about nine or ten, but he was to spend four more years in the village of the pine trunks.

After only one of those years he was disliked by all and by many feared, but it was difficult to put a finger on the trouble. He had picked up human language again, and most polite he was with it. If he saw a woman with a heavy load of washing he would offer to carry it, or the woodsman's axe, or he would help cut logs or feed chickens—though best he liked to wring their necks when they were due for the pot. You could never catch him in anything, yet it always seemed as if he had just been committing some unnatural and unwholesome act, or was just about to be as soon as your back was turned. Sometimes axes broke after Kernik had handled them: sometimes there were grubs in the stew after Kernik had gone by the door. The young woman frowned and muttered. They said the boy looked up their skirts, and, although this was doubtless normal enough, the way Kernik looked was different from the dirty, sniggering, natural way of other boys, though how, they could not exactly say, nor did they wish to, to be sure.

As for the children, they abhorred Kernik entirely. When in ones or twos they kept out of his way, but when three, four or more met him they would be braver, spit at him and make noises and sometimes throw stones. Whenever this happened, Kernik would run off as fast as his skinny legs would carry him. Safe among the pines or upon the rocks, he would quite literally lick his wounds, dry-eyed and solitary as a wolf. Sometimes he caught the children alone in the forest afterwards; and then he would twist their hair and whisper to them—bad things, evil things, things to be recalled in the dark with abject fear. These vengeances left no mark that could be seen. He was clever enough, Kernik was, in his own fashion. Besides, he could always get around the old woman, his foster-mother, with a whine, a bold smile, or one of those sidelong looks which obscurely, but entirely, terrified her.

The village had one particular god, the god of the mountain's black summit—Takerna. Once a month the old priest Voy would take the offerings of the villagers up the narrow track and leave them on the stone platform near the peak. Voy was a foolish old man, full of his own importance; full of rheumatism and grumbling, as well.

One dawn, just before the sun rose and lit Takerna's mountain, Voy was coming out of his house with the basket of bread-cakes, honey, and thin beer which he took to the god. And there, outside, stood the odd yellow boy from the forest, looking scrubbed and polished and obsequious.

"Father," said Kernik, bowing to the priest, "it's a long way for you to go with that heavy basket. Permit me the honor of accompanying you, and bearing your burden."

"Why, I don't know, boy. The peak is sacred to the god."

"Indeed, father, I have never doubted it. But it seems to me you should not have to go to him out of breath and weary. Someone of lesser importance than yourself should carry the offering and walk behind you."

These words appealed to the priest. So did the idea of other arms than his creaky ones taking the weight. So he agreed and, having spoken some words of warning on how the boy should behave—to which Kernik listened with most gratifying attention and deference—Voy handed over his basket and they set out.

Kernik was very careful. He stole nothing from the offering. He did not sneer at the priest behind his back as the other boys did. He helped him courteously on the steep parts of the track. He asked polite, intelligent questions about the ritual of the god. Once or twice, Voy, relieved of arm-ache and stimulated by the upper airs of the pine forest, cracked a few unamusing, stale jokes, and the boy laughed enthusiastically.

The priest waxed sentimental.

'What idiots they are in the village,' he thought. 'They don't try to understand the child, and simply because of his color which, while being quite peculiar, is only, after all, skin deep, ha, ha. He merely needs a little sensitive handling—such as I can exercise, being wise in such matters. Besides, I have never known one of the village boys to offer to help me, or to show me the proper respect which is my due.'

Presently they reached the last section of the journey, well above the trees, in a spot of particularly rugged and jumbled rock. The boy, who had been giving the priest his shoulder on which to lean, now came to a halt.

"Oh, father, I dare proceed no farther. We are only a few paces from the god."

Voy was put out. He could do with this strong wiry support right to the top.

"Have no fear, boy," he said magnanimously. "If you're with me, you will come to no harm."

Kernik thanked him sincerely, and, his fears apparently alleviated, aided the priest over the rough ground to the place where the stone platform stood.

While the priest held his ribs and panted, Kernik looked unobtrusively about.

It was not a high mountain, but this plateau, just under the peak, flattish and narrow, seemed pressed close to the enormous sky—a sky seldom blue, generally stormy, and livid now with a cold, grey-white upsurge of morning and the new sun the color of a healing wound. On every side the slopes fell back into a cloud of black-green pine trees, and far off, smoke rose to mark the village of trunks. In front of Kernik stood the altar, with a little roughhewn stone above it, barely resembling either deity or man. Kernik, who had already a sensitive nose for such things, could smell the emptiness of the peak. Surely no presence dwelled or even visited here? On the stone table lay the remains of last month's offering, but it was the ravens and the crows which had picked at it, not the god.

Shortly, Old Voy set out the fresh basket load, intoned a prayer, waved his arms desultorily, and turned round, obviously intending to start back at once.

"It's a very simple ritual," said Kernik, "and is that the god, Oh Father?"

"Hush. Yes."

"It is very old," said Kernik, "but rather weathered. Does he never ask for anything other than bread and honey?"

The priest eyed Kernik, slightly askance, but the boy seemed genuinely puzzled.

"For example, what?"

"Something alive," said Kernik. "Blood."

☀ 6 ☀

How the notion came to Kernik he was not sure. Perhaps, even then, there was some kind of sorcery in him, the gift of some ancestor from beyond the tall crags his saffron mother had crossed. At any rate, he was not one to pass up a chance however unlikely, however curious.

After that first excursion up Takerna's mountain, Kernik kept still, but he thought a great deal. The stones were very old, the carving older. Something had come there when the ritual had been more complex and strong and the gift more earnest.

He had gone with the priest merely in order to ingratiate himself to the old man, for Voy, the religious head of the village, might be useful later. But in so doing, Kernik had stumbled on an immutable truth, a truth older than the world. Priests claimed the gods made men, but this was not so. Men made the gods. Firstly, by forming them in clay, by chipping them from stone. Secondly, and more importantly, by *believing* in them, believing in them *utterly*.

During the month which followed, Kernik went to the priest's house four or five times. Each time he took something with him—a fish tickled from the stream for frying, bread stolen from the old woman's baking: "She thought you might be needing a fresh loaf," wood stolen from a yard: "I chopped it up this morning." Voy was impressed, flattered. He answered the boy's questions—all about the idol now. Almost without realizing he did so, the priest taught the boy the ritual—then the full ritual, more ancient than the village itself, the prayers the short-breathed priest never bothered with. Kernik's memory was like a knife; it pierced facts and held them. He missed not a word.

When the day came to go again, Kernik was there, as before, on the priest's threshold, waiting.

Together they climbed to the platform. The priest

52

gabbled the rite, set out the food, and they started down again. Then Kernik discovered he had left his neck scarf behind. Having taken it off to wipe his face after the climb, he had let it fall near the holy stone, actually on purpose. He begged the priest's pardon, entreated Voy to rest on a rock, for he would not be long, and hurried back.

The dark shadow of passing clouds fell on him as he emerged before the altar, alone. Then he felt it, or thought he did: something waiting.

He went close and stared into the blurred face of the idol.

"Takerna," he whispered, "Black Lord, High Lord, Wind Lord, Lord of Night and shadowed places. *They* forget, but your servant does not. I am your true priest, and I will return and worship you as it befits you to be worshipped." Then he knelt and bowed low, touching the earth with his forehead, and—did he imagine it?—felt a stirring on the air like a great invisible wing.

He escorted the priest back to the village, spoke respectfully to him, and said that now he must go and run errands for his kind, good foster-mother. But he ran to the forest instead, to hunt.

He caught, before the afternoon was at its height, three rabbits, and shut them into a little wooden cage he had made during the month of learning. Then he lay down under a tree, munched some bread and sausage he had taken, and slept, for he had a busy night ahead of him.

At sunset he was up and alert, and already making his way towards the summit of the mountain for the second time that day. He was a strong boy, for all his thinness. The manner in which he had lived had made him so.

It was full dark when he came up to the rough place below the altar, but he paused there, waiting for the moon to rise. The rabbits were nervous in their cage, as if they guessed, poor things, what was in store for them. Kernik paid them no heed. Animals and humans alike he treated with equal disdain. Only cats he had something of a liking for: he admired their independence, perhaps even their grace, but mostly their spite and their claws. Sometimes in the past, he had caught mice, and amused himself by putting them down in any village yard where a feline might be. How fascinating he found it, that immemorial game of cat and mouse.

Soon the moon did rise, a smoky moon with hollow eyes. Kernik picked up the rabbit cage and strode to the place of the idol.

Performed fully, the ritual was a long one, but Kernit dio not leave out a single phrase.

As the planets sailed over the sky, he spoke the words, made the gestures, obeised himself and kissed the feet of the stone. Finally he drew out a small hunter's knife he had thieved, and slit the neck veins of the rabbits. Their blood fell on the idol, anointing it, rich and black in the moonlight. Their carcasses he left it to devour. Then, kneeling again, his face on the altar, he said:

"Great Lord Takerna, I have done all as it should be done. I will raise you up and make you a god again, a mighty god to be feared and honored throughout the Korkeem, and the lands that lie thigh by thigh with her. But in order that I may do this, you in return must grant me some power. Gift for gift, Unconquerable One. Make me a Lord of men and I will make you King of the Earth."

All the passion, the boy's passion and the man's and the beast's, came trembling into Kernik's voice. His very soul seemed turned into a wedge of fire that thrust out through his lips in the form of the prayer. He shuddered all over, feeling a huge surge of yearning-made-power flood from him.

And, gazing at the image in the stars' paling, failing gleam, it seemed that the blurred face of the god was a little sharper, a little better defined, as if the weathering were falling away from it and the ancient strength returning.

Kernik crept down the mountain, exhausted with his travels and his vehemence: his hope, too.

Three days later he went back.

His heart pounded, for all that was left of the rabbits was a ball of fur and bones such as an owl might leave. Then he thought maybe a raven had done this, though it seemed unlikely. But going closer, he saw what little remained of the one raven that had tried to steal the idol's sacrifice.

Kernik threw himself at the feet of the stone in an ecstasy of joy, greed and triumph.

The will of Kernik was total. He had not known how total. He had made the idol live by means of it, and the idol appeared to reward him. He was clothed in the aura of the idol, the garment of its power. Now the children no longer threw stones. They sensed his new ability, and even when meeting him in groups of ten, they shrank away.

There began to be odd things. No one could understand it. The chickens might be busy in the yards when all at once they would cease pecking and burst out into the street, over walls, on to rain-butts, screaming and screeching as if the fox were after them. And who should be passing by but Kernik? Often the dogs would bark and jump and almost snap their chains, but nothing was there—except Kernik. A young girl, bathing in the stream below the village, saw a mauve-green goblin rise from the water to seize her, and ran all the way home without her clothes, and after her came Kernik, laughing, and eyeing her.

Some men went to see the priest.

"What nonsense about the boy. A good boy he is. *I* have no trouble with him," said Voy.

It was noticed that Kernik was often from home, from home also at night.

He was going to the idol once in every five days, as the old law had stipulated. Each time there was blood spilled. The stone was now black and shiny as jet, its features prominent, and even the horn it grasped and the runes cut into its breast, quite visible.

Then it came round to the day when the priest himself went up the mountain.

When he opened his door, there stood the yellow boy, waiting, as on the two previous occasions.

The priest had not said so to the men who came complaining, but he had been rather peeved himself, for not once this month had Kernik paid him a visit. However, the boy, without hesitation, spoke up.

"Honorable sir, how pleasant to see you. I have been unable to call, since my poor, kind foster-mother has been sick."

"I heard nothing of that," said the priest sharply.

"Well, there it is, you see," Kernik said sadly, "she will forever make light of her illness and tell no one."

The priest frowned, but the boy's eager deference soon won him over and, as before, they started together up the mountain, Kernik carrying the basket, the priest puffing along with one hand on the wiry shoulder.

It was a more tedious journey than Kernik had grown used to, for Voy was slow, but the prize was to come. It was a grey dawn, very overcast. They climbed up on to the plateau, and immediately the priest's jaw fell and his eyes oggled.

"Why—" he panted, "why, by the Mother— How can it be—?"

"One moment, if you please," said Kernik.

Going up to the idol, he bowed and kissed its blood-inky feet. Then he said to it:

"This time it isn't a rabbit, Black Lord. This time, as you see, it's a man. The false priest: the one who never bothered to attend you as you should be attended." Behind him, Kernik heard the priest begin to sputter like a too-fatty candle, but he went on loudly: "He's too large for me, Immense One. And the village will be also, without your help. Prove your influence, Lord of Lords. Take him yourself." And he prudently flung himself aside and flat to the rocky ground.

To begin with, it seemed nothing would happen. Kernik's guts turned crawling cold as worms in a grave, and he clutched the stones in his hands with clammy disappointment.

Then, sluggish at first, far off, came a sound like a dragon roaring, a dragon that bellowed in the mountain itself, not in the clouds above. And the sound grew, came nearer, enveloped the peak, the rocks; vibrated under Kernik's body. A flame scorched Kernik's eyes, not a white flame, but black—black as midnight, yet unbearably brilliant.

When Kernik's sight cleared, he found his nostrils were full of the smell of roasting flesh. There was a torch burning before the altar, a torch about the height of Voy.

Kernik came down the mountain.

He came down alone.

Overhead the sky was purple and shot with lightning.

Below, the village crouched in terror among the pines.

Dogs slunk under walls, birds huddled on posts.

Women offered prayers. Even the house demons sank deep into the foundations and groaned there.

No one quite knew why such fear had come on them, only knew they were afraid. Then Kernik came down the mountain.

Alone.

Kernik stood at the very center of the village. He threw up his bony yellow arms, and he laughed for pure malice and gratification. "I've won," said the laugh, "so watch out!" Aloud he shouted:

"The priest is dead. The black god Takerna has taken him. I am the new priest. Come and have a look."

And for some reason, though they would far rather not have come, out they streamed from every door. They stood there, pale as ashes, staring at the vile boy.

Then one man stirred, after him another, then another. They put their hands on mallets, axes, knives—whatever was near to them—and began to move in on him.

So Kernik created an illusion. It was not the first he had made. There had been the fox among the chickens, the rob-ber the dogs had leapt at, the water-goblin who had scared the naked girl. Kernik had discovered that this was the major talent the god on the mountain had released in him, and it was no mean gift. Now he used it to the full, clench-ing his brain like a fist, till the sweat ran into his eyes.

This is what the village saw:

Kernik grew. He grew to be eight feet tall. He wore purple and black, a robe made from the angry sky. All around him lashed lightning and white serpents with green venom drizzling from their mouths. This indeed was awful enough, but then something even more fearful took his place—a mighty wolf, black with scarlet eyes, a wolf tall as a horse, with its mouth open, a red rose spiked with sil-ver thorns.

The people fell back, fell to their knees. The men dropped their makeshift weapons. The women began to scream for mercy and the dogs to howl.

It was Kernik's moment of ultimate glory over the vil-lagers, his revenge for their mutterings, their jibes, their thrown stones, but, worst of all, for their unforgivable be-lief that he should be like them. When he turned his heavy, shaggy wolf's head towards his foster-mother, she who had taken him in and cared for him, he snarled and flaming saliva seemed to drip on the ground. The valves of the old woman's heart burst; in a few seconds she lay there dead, and Kernik exulted. The forest had not been kind to her after all.

Yet the powers were still adolescent in Kernik. It was a strain at that time to continue any illusion for very long.

Thus, when he felt he had them all where he wished them to be, he let the magic slide away and returned to his natural shape.

"You see," he said, "what I and my master, Takerna, can be like. Now you'll do as I say. Won't you?"

No one answered. No one denied him, either.

He and his god took charge.

When he was a little child, and he had coerced the visitors of the saffron whore, his mother, he had set them eccentric, useless tasks, mere symbols of their enslavement. Now, at thirteen, the tasks he set the village in the pines were also eccentric, irregular, but not without their uses; indeed no.

The rite of the god was celebrated now every third day. Between times, men of the village put snares in among the trees to catch forest creatures for sacrifice, and beer was brewed to be taken to the mountain and drunk in the sight of Takerna. For Takerna, or was it Kernik? loved the dark things: dark emotions and dark passions. Initially, the people were afraid, resentful. Then their legs grew accustomed to the climb, their natures—brutal of necessity— grew accustomed to the copious letting of blood, and their bellies grew accustomed to the strong drink. Not all, but many began to relax into this new and curious mode of life. Was it not good, that third night? Somehow, up on the plateau before the altar, Kernik—or the god—made them feel it was good—sinful, pleasurable, exciting. Drab routine had governed them almost from birth, for such was the law of survival. The forest enslaved them, the hearth, the seasons, the growing things, their beasts and their marriage partners. Here was tumultuous release. Soon the dancing and drinking became orgiastic beneath the staring peak. Women fell, crooning their lust, into the arms of men—any men—other women's husbands, or sons, or even their own sons, brothers and fathers. It did not matter. They served Takerna. He pardoned everything, rejoiced in every misdemeanor. In return, he sent them fine weather, plentiful crops, fish in the stream, sexual need and liquor—all were his bounty.

Takerna was the King, and Kernik was his prophet.

In the village street, passing him, they bowed to Kernik, as they had nodded to the priest. He was dreaded and blessed. They brought him presents, food, new garments. He led them up the mountain. It lasted all of a year.

The crops failed then. Of course they failed, for, in the anticipation of drunken delight and in its debilitated aftermath, the tillers of the soil had not been conscientious: had not broken their backs with the labor, as before. Chickens and goats had died—there had been a sickness. Children had died, a sickness also. When it turned cold, bitter snow clothed the mountain. The people began to regret, regret and forget, to rub their empty bellies, to long for the warm hearth and the full store and the old gods— undemanding and homely gods who asked only bread and a brief prayer.

They came to Kernik's door, the old woman's house where now he lived alone. They came reluctantly, looking at him under their lids. The room was full of animals in cages, full of excellent pies and cheeses the village had given him, full of the presence of Kernik, or the god. And Kernik had an answer to their difficulties. The god must be given something other than rabbits' blood and carnal rites, then he would help them again. What did the god want? Kernik would need to ask Takerna that. Go now, and in an hour's time be ready for the reply.

As it turned out, what Takerna wanted was a maiden sacrifice, a virgin slain on his altar.

By now, to the villagers, also in actual fact, Kernik and Takerna were virtually synonymous, and not only in their names. Each was a symbiote, the black stone and the yellow boy, and neither could exist without the other. The god needed Kernik to spark his dark power. Kernik needed the god to spark the dark power in himself. So their aims and desires were at one. Kernik wanted the sacrifice himself, and thus the god wanted it. Yet also, it was the god's wish that had inspired the boy.

Kernik had no sexual urge, no virility, no physical manhood, and never would have. All his drive was mental. His brain had absorbed the great potential magic energy of his groin, and harnessed it forever in the service of other things. When he had looked at women, it was only with a contemptuous fascination—because they were not made as he was.

It was death and killing which at this time filled Kernik with ecstasy, not of the senses or the flesh, but to the limit of his pitiless mind. When his knife plunged into the maiden, he would experience the complete orgasm of dominance.

He told the village the god's word, standing in the frosty street with all his ability of illusion on him. He chanted the message to them, he hypnotized them and made them agree. They were to draw the girl by lot.

He watched with greedy eyes, his mouth moistening. A cry went up, a mother fell down weeping. The daughter was led out, white as bleached linen, her eyes like charred glass.

Night came, and he took them up Takerna's mountain. Torches blazed like red flowers in their hands and made the snow red underfoot.

They came to the altar and the girl was laid down. She made no sound, but tossed her head from side to side like a sleeper in the grip of a nightmare. Men held her wrists. The torches crackled. The moon rose. Kernik stood over her with his sharp knife, speaking soft, and lovingly, to the idol.

Then it happened. Suddenly. It took only a minute— less, for Kernik's kingdom to fall.

There was a young man who had been betrothed to the girl. Three years before he had thrown stones at Kernik and, even through the bewitchment, part of him had not forgotten his aversion to the yellow boy with the slinking untrustworthy ways. Now, loving his girl, wanting to protect her, all the passion in the youth came bubbling to the surface. He gave a hoarse yell and, leaping between the torches and over the altar, he seized Kernik's hand that held up the knife.

Kernik, strong as whipcord in his narrow skin, twisted and writhed but could not quite get free. Just as his wrist was about to snap, he let go the knife and reached out instead towards the black stone that was Takerna.

A ruddy light was playing over it, more than the torches. A rumble came from underfoot.

"Oh, my High Master—" Kernik began, but he got no further.

The face of the young man was mad with terror now, as well as fury. He had the look of an animal at bay, the same snarling demented willingness to meet the ring of hunting spears, the fangs of the dogs— He thrust past Kernik, straight to the carved idol, and grasped it in his arms.

The stone was separate from the altar; it could be moved, though it was heavy. The youth tottered backwards, grappling the idol as if he wrestled something of sentient flesh. He gave a crow of victory, and the torches burst in his great eyes. He mouthed the girl's name, and she sat up on the altar, and stared at him, bemused. The crowd held its breath. Only Kernik shouted—an unintelligible, bestial sound, half imprecation, half command. But the young man was turning now, turning towards the lip of the plateau where the mountain jumped off into rolling slope, jagged boulders, spinning space. . . . He raised his arms, the idol in them. He meant to throw it down, smash it on the rocks beneath.

His girl screamed, high and shrill as a bird.

The idol toppled, it fell.

Somehow, the youth was falling with it. He made no sound. His face receded down the distance, staring white, eyes staring red, the idol held tight as a lover to his breast.

Far below, one large outcrop of stone jutted up from among the smoky steeples of the pine trees. Here the youth and the idol crashed together.

There was an explosion, a shattering concussion. Black stars erupted on black air. Splinters of stone showered upwards and rained down again like hail. The villagers plunged on their faces, covering their heads. The mountain grumbled deep within itself, and then grew still.

Altogether, a great stillness followed, a vast quiet. The atmosphere seemed deadened, as if some vibrant life had gone out of it forever.

Kernik lay across the altar from which the maiden had fled, and he wept.

He wept at the desolation and emptiness he felt in every fibre. The life had gone from him also. His very bones seemed drained of marrow. The god had died, and the powers of Kernik had died with him.

Presently, trapped under the bowl of inanimate deafness that had upturned over the mountain, a figure rose like a shaft of pale steam—Kernik's virgin sacrifice, the girl for whom the youth had died. She was in the grip of that extraordinary cold hysteria which comes between one raging paroxysm of anguish and another.

She pointed at Kernik, lying there, tears running from his eyes and nostrils, impotent, disrobed of his splendor.

"You die, too," she said. "Filth. Devil."

One by one, all about, men and women got up, their faces washed colorless and their mouths open to get breath. They realized now how they had been put to his use. They dismissed the pleasure of their sins, remembering only the reckoning—the hollow store, the dead children, the harsh teeth of winter already fastened on their throats. The spell dropped from them. Vengeance warmed their frozen veins. Hands crept to knives, groped for stones, as before. This time Kernik could not summon an illusion to clothe his nakedness.

Only the limber quickness of Kernik saved him, his flexible, slight body and feet agile as hands.

He fled down the mountain. He fled through the village. Hot-eyed, they came after him, slipping and rolling on rocks and snow, their torches smearing purple, orange, silver as they ran.

Kernik reached the forest and darted into it. His lungs blazed with unimaginable fires, but his limbs kept on as if independent of organs or brain. Sometimes, though far off, he saw torchlight ravage the trees, or heard their shouts, the brazen voices of dogs.

He came to a wide stream, not entirely frozen, and dashed down it, smashing the ice with his hands and feet, presumably losing his scent, for after this, the dog noises faded.

It seemed he ran, or half ran, all night. Near dawn he shambled across a blue landscape between the tall poles of the trees. His eyes were glazed, his tongue lolled like a wolf's and saliva came from his open mouth. Now the forest was thinning out; he barely noticed. A wall of rock; a dark opening—shelter. He crawled into it, and fell forwards on his face.

The hunters did not find him that day, nor any day, though they searched for three or four. The village felt a curse had fallen on it. It returned to labor in a spirit of frantic expiation. The girl—Kernik's maiden—hanged herself. The snow came again, that white unwelcome visitor, and many died, of starvation or of the cold. The mountain became a place of evil reputation which no one visited, and the pines wailed below in the wind.

* 7 *

Kernik lay in the cave one day, one night. When he emerged—stiff, famished—huge white plains lay before him in the pale winter sun.

Thin snow was down now everywhere, like salt.

Kernik rubbed his limbs for warmth. Later he caught an unsuspecting rabbit, in the old fashion, like a cat, and ate it as of old: raw, spitting out the fur and the bones. He reverted to his original ways quite easily, those grizzly skills he had learned in the forest when he was ten years of age.

But there was no going back. He had known power, and the wine of sorcery had intoxicated him. He was fourteen but he looked older. Exposed dreams, like lacerated nerves, tortured his heart, such as his heart was. But there was no answer and no salve. Sometimes he would bite his own flesh to end these memories.

All that winter he dwelt on the great plains, catching and eating his food, and adapting his clothing from the skins of the things he caught. He had found another cave. He lived in it like the wolf he frequently resembled and, in wolf fashion, with a hide of stolen fur and without fire, cracking bones with his spiked teeth.

Spring came bright as a green flame. Kernik did not value it or the golden stars of flowers that grew in the grass and about his stony door. But he set off, moving towards the distant shadow of hills. Soon it was warm enough to sleep on the gold flower stars, under the silver ones above.

Then he found the robbers' camp.

Not that he knew them for robbers.

There were two brown tents, five tethered ponies, a fire with a roast being turned over it. It was early dusk; a soft transparent afterlight covered the world. The smell of the cooked meat was enticing to Kernik, for he had grown to enjoy such food in the pine-trunk village. He planned to steal something, but did not get far. The robbers, following

the trade they did, had set a look-out. Abruptly Kernik
was discovered, seized, and taken down the slope.

He made no protest. He had learned a few things—caution, flattery.

An enormous man came from the second tent. He was
immensely fat, yet strong as an ox. His eyebrows curled,
and his moustaches, and his thick lips. He had one earring
of corrupt silver.

Here was the chief of the camp, Kernik guessed uner-
ringly. He bowed.

The chief laughed. He liked the look of Kernik: vicious,
uncanny, wiry—thin enough to squeeze in and out of narrow windows.

Kernik lived and roved with the chief's band five years
in all, across the length and breadth of the Volkyan Plain.
He changed his name to suit the place, as before he had
taken his name from the black god. Now he was Volk. He
wore his hair in a plait as did the chief's four men, he acquired a copper earring. He indulged all his dark passions—his lust for killing and inflicting pain, his love of
cruel jokes, his contempt for humanity at large, his greed
for good things—all the dark passions save one. The chief
trusted him, the chief gave him command of the thieves'
work, when he himself was lolling in some woman's house,
drinking or in bed. Kernik Volk was cunning and clever;
he said little; he was chiselled and burnished by suppressed
unknowable desires.

But, oh, the rat gnawed forever at his heart. Once he
had been the anointed of a god. Once he had been a
prophet eight feet tall, a wolf, a devil, a magician and
master of illusion. When he killed now, he thought on
these things. The knife spoke from his frustration. He slew
again and again, in the persons of merchants, soldiers, un-
wisely talkative whores, the boy who had leaped from the
mountain with Takerna in his arms. And so Kernik came
to sate his joy in killing, for he found it did not, after all,
appease him. He wanted to destroy but not precisely to
kill, and he had no power, no power to do anything.

Sometimes he saw temples in the towns, full of gods,
but never the black god, his genius. Often in those five
years, deep in the grim bowel of the night, he would wake,
he would strive to recapture his ability. But without the

god it was not to be done. So he learned a fresh lesson, learned how to bear the unbearable thing.

However, there were other lessons in store for him.

There was one large sprawling town on the plains of the Volkyan, a town of stone built on the bank of a river called Wide. The name of the town was Svatza. From the towers of its three temples at noon, and midnight, and dawn bells sounded: and in it there was one very rich man whom the robbers had for some time been intending to visit.

No luck lasts forever. The unloved goddess finally caught up with them; Lady Misfortune. The rich man had sniffed the air, had laid a trap. In the fighting, the chief's four men died, and he himself was hanged in the broad square of Svatza on the stroke of the noon bell. Kernik Volk was condemned to another sort of death, a longer one. He was sent to the renowned dungeon of Svatza, the pitchy, water-running sewer that lay below the river itself; from which rarely anyone returned, and those who did, with bodies nerveless as the walls, and brains sodden as the sponges that grew on them.

Little light penetrated Svatza jail. There was just enough for the melanic rats and the albino frogs to see by. In places, water rose to three feet or higher. You could hear no bells, but the sound of water was always present, the dripping of it, the hissing of it. At first it seemed to soak through your ears into your mind. Later, you no longer heard it.

The prison was divided into cells, rough made from the mud and debris of the banks, shored up with pillars of rusty iron. Sometimes walls subsided, shrieking men were buried and gradually silenced.

Once every fourteen days soldiers of the governor of Svatza would stroll through the dungeons, between the cells, casting stale bread and half-rotten chunks of meat to the creatures there. For drink they had the stagnant water from the walls. Often there was sickness and death. Here and there forgotten men sat pale as curd, blind and witless, singing or whispering.

The first three days in his cell, Kernik raged. He had taken on the temperament of a robber and cut-throat. He pummelled the walls and screamed. A dim rumbling of hate and despair from all about answered him, dehumanized as the voice of the river itself.

Eventually he fell quiet. The languor of that living tomb began to creep over him.

Then he saw a luminous frog squatting against the far wall. For an instant the circumstances were put aside. Kernik tensed and sprang. So quick he was that he had the frog, and presently devoured its bitter flesh, more wholesome, despite its flavor, than the offerings of the soldiers. Afterwards, he caught other things.

Kernik resumed his old life yet again.

The water did not dull his senses, only lulled them. Outwardly he grew dumb and pallid. Inwardly his mind began to discover its own deep kingdom. He travelled those roads of his soul he had never seen before, grappling forever as he had been with external things. He prayed also, long, long prayers. He repeated the words of the magic rite he had offered the god on the mountain. "Takerna, Revered Master, help me, save me, and we shall be one again, Kings again, you and I."

He had no actual hope. It was ritual merely, the product of his fierce brain turned entirely upon itself.

Time passed. Much time. Years. Maybe ten, maybe twenty of them. Time loses itself in dungeons, particularly in the river dungeon of Svatza. A man grew old, whatever age he had been to begin with; unearthly old. His skin shrivelled, his bones warped, his face pleated like cloth. Age is only a ruination of the flesh, a wearing of the spirit. Both these processes Svatza supplied. No longer could the age of Kernik be given with any certainty.

Kernik the prophet, Kernik the robber. Kernik Volk, eater of frogs, chanter of prayers. His yellow skin was bleached now ash white as the dead boughs of an aspen tree. His finger nails grew long and black.

He dwelled with himself, and survived it. He knew himself as very few are given to know.

One day the door of his cell opened. Just like that.

A torch shone in, hurting his eyes.

"Stand up, you scum," shouted the voice of a soldier— he knew all their voices well by then. Kernik rose. "See," the soldier went on, proudly, smugly, "did I not insist, Lord Overseer, that this one is strong and tough. Mother Earth knows how long he's been here, but he still understands an order, and his limbs are quite supple. You. Open your mouth, let the lord see your teeth. See, Lord Overseer,

he's kept them all. Fresh meat he gets. He catches the
rats and eats them, I've seen him do it. Quick as a cat,
he is. Did I not insist?"

Kernik glimpsed, through dazzled running eyes, a
shadow nodding, next to the silhouette of the soldier.

"Out," the soldier said. "Yes, you. Quick. Before someone changes his mind."

It transpired that the old Duke of the Korkeem had
died, and a new Duke reigned in Arkev. The new Duke
planned that three new towers of white stone be added to
the palace there, and the quarries of this stone lay on the
Volkyan west of Svatza among the hills.

It was a wind-pared upland place. The stone was in
steep banks, hard blocks held in by layers of more friable
material. The labor was harsh, the climate uncharitable.
Men fell from the uncertain scaffolding, the others, soon
also to expire, their lungs clogged by the fine white powder
that burst from the soft areas of the quarry walls at every
blow of the pick. Only slaves and felons were sent to this
work, the expendable detritus of the community, and only
the strong ones at that. Some lived two years in the quarries, towards the end spitting pink phlegm; a weak man
would not last much above two months.

Kernik, the robber who had survived Svatza jail, was an
ideal candidate.

Dragged out into the acid brillance of the blinding sun,
a sun from which he had been hidden for that uncountable stasis of years, the world showed itself to him all one
wincing intolerable flame.

Chained ankle to ankle, waist to waist, wrist to wrist,
with fifty others, he was herded from the town, along
broad roads, slender uneven trackways, over the ford of
the swirling river. Yearning for night, cool on the eyes.
Not yet glad to be in the air. Sores from the chains, sores
on his face from the water which streamed from his eyes
and nostrils. A hunk of bread once a day. No chance to
catch anything, chained as he was. Like one great desolate
sea of bewildered agony, drowning him. Only the inner
communion of brain with thoughts to solace him, a clear
cold voice speaking gently to him, as if to an idiot.

They came to the quarries.

The hills were the color of winter without the snow,
milked almost dry of their riches. A white fog hung above

the workings, soft as swans' down on the rim of the hard, blue-grey sky.

A fragment of black bread, a scoop of water. The unchaining. At last each man free of his fellow, only a piece of rope fixed between his iron anklets, enough slack to walk, not enough to run.

Kernik lay on his belly. His eyes were clearer now. Up on the bleak hillside he saw a twitch and flicker in the grass. Rabbits?

The soldiers were eating beef and drinking red wine. Kernik began to inch up the slope, fraction by fraction. The rope made no noise, that was good. There was a rock on the hill, about two feet high, a dark, odd-looking rock. If he could reach it, it would partially shelter him from the soldiers' eyes while it waited for the rabbit to show itself again.

Kernik reached the rock. He reached his destiny and for a moment did not know it.

Then there came a humming in his head. His brain spoke to him. Look. Kernik looked, upwards. A stone hand grasped a stone horn, above it, a face cruel as an eagle's, black as jet, looked down into his, familiar and beloved as the tender countenance of a mother.

Kernik lay there, grasping the feet of the idol. He sobbed, his body shook; no tears came, they were spent.

"Takerna, Takerna, my Lord, my adored Master, Black Immortal One, answer to my prayers."

No ritual now, no hint of courtesy, it was true rapture spilling from Kernik. And far, far away, there came a tremor, surely, under his touch.

Then a blade of white teeth tore across his back.

"Up! Take your hands away." Kernik rolled over, came to his feet trembling. The whip coiled back now like a snake over his arm, the overseer stood grinning at him. "Religious, are you? Praying were you? I'll give you something to pray about shortly."

"Takerna," Kernik said, actually to the god, but the overseer spat.

"Backlands name. Oh, most ignorant bastard, I will tell you, this little fellow has a little house in Arkev for all his primitive and uncouth aspect. But I doubt if the Duke bothers with him. The Sun and the Moon and the Stars are the gods of the cities. There is a golden-roofed temple in Arkev, dedicated to the Sun, and at noon the god's chariot may be seen resting upon the exact point of the highest dome. Though you'll never see it, dreg."

"Takerna," Kernik said again.

"No," said the overseer, "Sovan, as he is named in the Duke's city. Sovan Tovannazit. Big name for small item. Now, down the blasted hill before I skin you, weasel."

Kernik obeyed. He staggered and once fell. The overseer flicked him with the whip, for diversion. Kernik felt a strange dark radiance go with him, warmer than the sun, black light that did not torture his eyes—the presence of the god.

Here, in this second effigy with the city name, the being of Takerna had yet remembered his priest.

Kernik was driven back to his place, and not long after, with the others, into the smoking pallor of the quarry. But he swung the pick lustily, as if he loved the white stone and was ardent to release it. The sun was low; amber shadows streamed down the hills and the evening wind began to grind its teeth. Kernik grinned as he worked, grinding his own.

A wonderful electric excitement moved up and down over his ill-treated body, a balm to wounds on flesh and on heart.

Just about sunset, he turned to the man beside him, a burly giant, thick with hair. Kernik looked, and thought. He clenched his brain like a fist, as he had done before, and he felt the aura of the god build there, in him and all around him. The hairy man let out a yell and jumped sideways, his eyes—veiled and bitter eyes—momentarily naked with alarm. Kernik had made him see something in the quarry wall, something that had no business there, maybe a dragon's jaws or a leaping beast. The proximity of Takerna had reawakened power.

Kernik threw back his head. He howled madly, composite delight and fury. A whip came down once, twice, thrice on his shoulders. He did not care. Soon it would be night.

Night, the dark widow, came walking on the hills.

In the huts, toil suspended, men shivered and cursed and tumbled into deadly sleeps. Kernik kept awake. His eyes shone with a vague animal redness like dying coals. He saw very well without the sun.

Two soldiers sat outside, dicing. Kernik looked at them

intently. Suddenly both men jumped up, saluted and ran off. They thought they had seen an officer and received an order, and now the doorway of Kernik's hut was empty.

Kernik stole out. Like a shadow he went, and the rising moon cast a second shadow away from him on the rough ground.

Easy to prowl up the slope of the hill, leaving behind the quarry, the big lighted house of the soldiers.

He reached the idol. He lay down at its feet, his lips on the stone. Then, kneeling, he began to recite the ancient words, all perfect, not one forgotten.

He arrived at the moment when the offering was to be made. He felt the stone waiting under his hands. He had no creature to kill, but it did not matter. Kernik had realized what was needful, the ultimate spell that would bind him irrevocably to the god—he had been too impetuous, too untried, to understand before.

The blood he spilled must be his own, the sacrifice himself. Somehow he knew instinctively this death was not a death, that what came after was his goal, had always been so.

He had not been able to discover a weapon, for such things were kept well out of the reach of the quarry slaves. But then, this savage act had a rightness to it, the seal upon the giving.

He did not mind the pain, gnawing through the artery on his wrist as the wolf gnaws through its leg in order to get free of the trap. Pain was nothing. His blood leapt towards the idol of its own volition, and the hillside sank away.

Kernik lay in blackness, and fiery claws rent him, and a silver beak gouged him, but they rent and gouged him with a sort of love, and with a sort of love he suffered them. Then came colors and dreams, and a great wind blowing through the shell of him, so that he knew that he was empty. Last, the god came. There are no words for that.

When he opened his eyes, the sun was rising. The beautiless hills were briefly and patchily shining, as if struck from impure gold.

Kernik rose, stretched, stared straight into the sun itself, as only eagles can stare.

He *felt* the power. Oh, he felt it. Not clothing him now, but part of him.

He looked at his hands, bloodless white as the stone of the quarry. He smiled, and put on them rings of silver and gold. He dressed his body in a robe the shade of storms, embroidered twenty times with the face of the sun. He found that he did not need to trouble with the illusion; once made, it held itself in place without help from him, until he chose another. He looked back at the statue of Takerna.

At first it shocked him, the black rubble which the god had become, but only at first, before he understood. Then he glanced about where the sun was pouring, searching for something which he did not find. Not over rock, not over grass, even in the glare of the morning.

Kernik no longer cast a shadow.

In the place of huts below, men were stirring. Two soldiers pointed up at him; next, the overseer came out.

Let them see what I am, eh, my dearest of all lords?

Kernik raised his arms. They were wings. Lifted his head. It was a bird's cruel, hooked mask. Kernik was a falcon, and the falcon flew up into the air, up into the blue, wide air above the hills.

Among the huts, they shouted, pointed and ran.

In the air the falcon screamed derisively.

More than illusion now, it was reality. For Kernik flew with feathers on his back, Kernik-Takerna-Volk flew with the sun in his sideways eyes, high over the husk of the black god and the humility of the golden land, and the magician Volkhavaar was born.

* 8 *

Two other things happened that year of Volkhavaar and the black god.

In the great slave market of a town far to the west of the Korkeem, a seven-year-old girl was put up for auction and presently sold. Raiders from a ship-wrecked vessel had brought her there, not kindly men. Her hair was long and raven-dark, her eyes the color of foxes. She was thin as a bone from the cruelty and the voyage, from sorrow and from fear, but she stood there straight and grim as the bitterest woman of the bluest blood has ever stood in chains after some war.

"Do you know your name, wench?" her new owner snapped at her.

"Shaina, by your leave," she proudly and politely answered him.

Off to the north, there was a white mansion in a wealthy town where the nobleman Parvel lived with his wife and his one, two, three, four, five sons.

When your father has five sons, maybe it is not so bad. Not so bad if you are the first son, certainly, nor so bad even if you are the second or the third. If you are the fourth, perhaps your chances are more slender. If you are the fifth son, then, no doubt, there is too much salt in your dish.

Dasyel Parvelson was thirteen years of age, a thin, dark and well-mannered boy, with a face, even then, that made the girls turn round and some of the boys pick fights. But Dasyel was easy-going and even-tempered for the most part, with a quick ear and a good memory for songs and stories—an ability he had not yet seen the worth of—and few shadows in his brain and heart. Except for the shadows of dreams, where the shade thickened somewhat. It was not so much a sense of personal uniqueness he wanted, not a desire to prove himself, be one alone and

above the rest; merely, he wished to know his own road.
For the fifth son of a rich man there was little to do, small
challenge and no pretense at ambition. He did not dislike
his brothers, so was not inspired to pray for a plague to
carry them off, and leave hearth, money-bags and respon-
sibility to him. Thus, from an early age, a bit of him had
been gazing outwards, beyond his father's white house, the
town, the forests and hills, towards any horizon that might
say to him: Dasyel, here is a horse that only you can ride.

One day, the horse rode over the horizon, into the town.

Many itinerants came and went: holy men, priests of
the sun dressed in scarlet, or simply grey-robed accolytes
of obscure faiths. Healers and physicians with wonder
cures for toothaches, and impotence, traders with furs and
beads, ballad singers—of special interest to Dasyel—with
their wild eyes and one-stringed instruments strapped on
their backs. This day, however, late in spring, it was a
troupe of actors.

They put on a show by night in the market place. The
leader of the troupe rapped on the ground with his staff of
pealed wood. Torches flared on poles, lighting fantastically
the rainbow clothes, the gold sun-masks and silver moon-
masks, the curving swords with glass gems in the hilts
gleaming emerald and topaz.

The whole town and all the five sons of Parvel were
there, looking on. The two eldest sons lolled in front of the
tavern on chairs brought out for the purpose. The third
and fourth ogled the three actresses. The fifth son, having
been told he must be home and not present in such a
crowd and so late, was up on the tavern roof.

There was a song. The youngest actress sang it. A big
brown man accompanied her on a pipe. She was about fif-
teen, and smote a green zither delicately, her voice thin
but sure as a bird's. Dasyel fell in love with her a little,
but it was more than that. That song had to do with freedom, with the wide highway that crossed the Korkeem
and beyond it, the actor's country, which had no bound-
aries. Somewhere during the song, a voice said to Dasyel:
Here I am. Your road. Take me, or I shall be lost forever.

The answer to the dream had been there a long while,
but he had not known it. Now he thought of his father's
house, his father, his mother, the brothers . . . and saw
only childhood, which was over already. It is as easy to be

alone with six kin as it is to be alone by yourself, and maybe easier.

So, when the actors rode from the town, near dawn, in their painted carts, Dasyel went after, and came up with them about ten miles and one sunrise later.

The leader of the troup, Jy by name, was a fierce bearded man with four shrewish wives, each safely distant at the four points of the compass.

"Be off, you young fool," he shouted when he saw Dasyel. "Do you suppose this a charitable institution?"

"No, sir," said Dasyel promptly, "I'll earn my bread any way you think fit. I can look after your ponies, pack and unpack your gear—oh, and I'm very good at talking round difficult innkeepers. My brothers, you understand, taught me that."

"Are you, by the Hot Belly of Mother Earth Underfoot and may I be damned? You've enough to say now, at any rate. Besides which, you speak like a well-brought-up, well-educated wretch of an aristocrat."

"So I am," said Dasyel, "but anyone can learn new ways."

"Ho! Someone's been at the knife-grinder's till he's *nice* and sharp," roared Jy, not at all displeased, and laughed. He could see at a glance, could the showman, that this handsome boy had a face that might increase the crowds, particularly given a couple of years, and a voice in the bargain, obviously early broken and with the sound of it of some dark clear metal. "Can you sing, you runaway?" Jy demanded.

"Poorly," said Dasyel.

"Oh, modest now, are we?"

"I have not been trained."

"Nor to act, I hazard, but you think you can do that."

Dasyel smiled, and the leader could foresee what that smile would do to a market full of women.

"Let me hear you say," said Jy, "the ballad of Seeva and the Hill of Glass."

Perhaps he thought the nobleman's son did not know such a popular tale. If so Dasyel surprised him.

Jy sat in his cart, his leader's staff across his knees, a cup of wine in his hand, listening. Not a blush from the lad, and he recited well, confound him, and look at the girls, tough girls of the road who should know better, all eyes, the minxes.

"Enough," Jy said. "You're not bad. For a nobleman's brat. A bit too flowery, but a few nights with a hollow gut in the rain, and a few beds with fleas in 'em will cure you of that. You'll look after the ponies, like you said. And you'll fetch and carry, and get a clip round your ears if you're not good at it. In six months, maybe I'll let you loose on a crowd. If they don't tear you to pieces, maybe you're one of my troupe."

Nine years Dasyel travelled in that company.

Sometimes it altered a little; someone would see a troupe going in a direction—geographical or dramatic— that appealed to him more, and leave Jy's carts to travel with theirs; a girl might marry, a young man get sick of the road and take up a trade in preference, an old man die. All these things happened. Conversely, other actors came to join them. There were the stalwarts, too, Jy's regulars. Roshi, for one, a sun-burned fat man, all good humor and a headful of melody; his fingers full of songs which poured like silver water from a pipe set to a smiling mouth. Roshi, the ever-kind, finding a draggled sparrow on the path, setting its broken wing, healing and letting it go; Roshi, nursing an inn-woman's baby; Roshi telling a girl with a crippled foot she had a face like flowers and adding, thereby, a drop of sweetness to the bitter pool of her life. And always, there was Jy himself: jovial, bristling, hard and sound as a nut, except when there was too much liquor in a tavern.

Also on the highway of those years were failure and success, lovers, quarrels, a brawl or two, friendships, trouble; girls with bright eyes, parts with tricky phrases, props lost, ponies stolen, wheels that came off carts, and all the empty guts, rainy nights and flea-bitten beds Jy had promised him.

Dasyel was actor—flesh, bone, blood—inside a year. He had the knack of it, more than the art of learning words and gestures, more than a handsome face. He had all the light and shade, all the sorcery that his roaming and uncertain career required. He stuck with Jy because Jy was his father. His true father, that is—his creator. Jy taught him his profession, and besides, needed some looking after. There were the four wives, for one; the wine-shops for another.

And the road was as wide as Dasyel had known it would be.

He crossed mountains and rivers, hills and forests. He saw seas pale blue as smoke, and seas dark indigo with fury. Taverns he saw, cities. He saw the Temple of the Sun and the Temple of the Moon in Arkev. Maybe he passed the little dark house of Sovan Tovannazit, and never noticed.

The tracks of men's lives go every way.

One day when he was acting a warrior, and breaking hearts in some village under a cold hill, a black-haired slave girl was throwing grain to chickens. One night, when he was with a pretty woman in some western town, the girl with black hair was lying for the first time under Old Ash's roof, her ears smarting from the first of the many blows Old Ash's wife would deal her.

And one noon, when Shaina was washing clothes in the stream of the goats' pasture, and Dasyel and Roshi between them shoeing a pony, eastwards, on the edge of Volkyan Plain, Volk Volkhavaar stood at a high window, casting no shadow and thinking his own thoughts, or the thoughts of his black god.

✳ 9 ✳

Those nine years, while Dasyel the young actor had travelled the roads, and Shaina the slave had toiled in foreign houses, Kernik Volk Volkhavaar had been garnering life, getting back for himself the juicy goodness of it.

Nine years were not excessive to him. He knew his lifespan, reborn from the god, would be long, almost indefinite. He was not immortal, even his god had not really been that, but he was enduring. Neither was he all-powerful, though to some, in those nine years, he seemed to be.

Master of Illusion, Shape-Changer, Deceiver of Minds.

No, not all-powerful, not Volkhavaar. He could not do everything. Only make it seem he could.

At first, drunk with his freedom from various chains, jails, deprivations, he had lived everywhere and nowhere about the plains of the Volkyan. Sometimes he would stride into a lonely village, seemingly dressed in the scarlet of a sun priest, and out the food and the drink would come. He took a delight in that, the way they brought him the best of their store, these people who, when he was adolescent and yellow of skin, would have sneered and beaten him if they could. He loved to fool them after, by casting that spell of illusion and deception that made them forget him, recollect instead a band of robbers or gang of similar ruffians who had seized their food by force. Often he went back to the same place seven days in a row, each day greeted freshly, unremembered, and the store brought out again— "This is all we have left, blessed father. Thieves took the rest." He stripped them all, laughing up his sleeve, now a scarlet sleeve, now purple. He had always liked cruel jokes. He never tired of that one.

Darker things he did. He changed shape—falcon, wolf, black horse, lead-green fish-king of the Wide River. Maybe that was illusion too, illusion that convinced not only bystanders but also, in some curious physical way, himself. Maybe all the while it was Volk the man who sprang on

77

the lamb, and gutted it with his long lupine teeth, Volk the man who only seemed to hunt the little fish in the river deeps. But as far as he knew he filled his belly, tasted warm blood and cold, flew and stooped across the sky on slender, strong falcon wings, danced on his hind limbs under the moon, black horse with a voice of harsh silver. Who knew? If the illusion is quite perfect, who is to say it is not real?

A piece of stone he had taken from the rubble of the black god above the quarry. He wore it, to begin with, around his neck on a cord. He made it glow and shine and the cord resemble gold. It was his talisman, the conductor of the power in him.

For there were still limits. He only found them gradually. He still needed the aura of the god.

If ever he chanced to forget Takerna, the presence of Takerna which had devoured his blood and his shadow and poured into him, in exchange, the energy held in the stone, Volk's power faltered. Perhaps the weakness was only in himself, that he did not trust himself enough, lacked faith in what he had become. Whatever it was, he deemed it prudent, presently, whenever he spoke a condition or a spell or created an illusion, to do so in the name of Takerna his master and his genius. It was his crutch. All men, even men without shadows, the magician-priests of Darkness, need a higher lamp than their own light— someone to entreat, someone to thank, someone to bear the burden of their heavy deeds.

At last Volk Volkhavaar came to live in a tower of rock, an old watch post above the Wide River.

Somedays it would look like a ruin, with ravens swarming round it, then again like an outcrop of the rocky hill itself. At various times travellers going by below, strangers, would see in the distance a spire of silver with a dome of gold, crystal windows, emerald doors—"Who lives *there*, by the Mother?" "Hush, don't ask his name. He is called the Black Horse or Lord Wolf. He steals from our flocks, he draws away our young maidens and tramples them with iron hooves. Be merciful, great one." And, at the hill's foot, an offering of loaves, wine, fish, meat.

How do magicians live? How do they spend their days, lacking nothing or little? What are their dreams, if any? When a road is very dark it is hard to see the milestones on it.

Sometimes, from that high tower on the Volkyan, he would hear a pick strike, off over the hills, from the quarries that had almost been his destiny. White stone for Arkev. One day Arkev would know him. There was a black flower waiting to grow in him from the seed of that slavery. He never forgot how the overseer derided his god, the mention of the neglected temple in bright sun and moon shadow. Since he wasted virtually nothing, the magician understood that every impulse he gratified now would somehow pave his way to that place.

His impulses. He had grown tired of killing in the robbers' service, and still that need gnawed in him to destroy. So it came about that he began to destroy things and people in other ways, experimenting to see which satisfied him the most. Forms of torture he quickly set aside. Basically indifferent to human pain, he had early exhausted the titillation he got from it. Mental hurt interested him more, but not entirely; the wounded heart was vocal, it found words. Some part of Volk wished to eradicate all words and thoughts from others. The slaves that did his bidding must be only that, characterless, colorless, alive only with the life he briefly lent them. Already he would invent things out of the air—beasts and birds, demons to frighten and entice. But they were shadows. Imagine human men and women, locked up in rooms, lying there limp and discarded as toys, waiting for his voice. Human slaves that anyone might touch, embrace, caress; things that breathed with the breath of life, ate real food, had flesh susceptible to wounds, to pleasure, but were still entirely dependent on the will of the magician. . . .

So he came to it.

Like a strange, intense and wicked child, he began to collect a cupboard full of dolls. He took only the best.

A maiden he saw by the town of Yevdor.

A falcon, he perched on the hill, and watched her. She carried two clay pots to the stream. She filled them. She washed her hair. Her hair was yellow, the color of gold in the sun. Pretty, pretty. Another might have desired her. The wolf wanted her flesh, the horse to bear her away screaming on his back, through the black claws of pines, to the abyss where he would shake her off. Volkhavaar wanted to lead her by a chain of opals, to see how other men stared hotly at her, to say: "She is mine and I am indifferent to her, yet see how she does everything I tell her, how, when I am from home, she lies blank-eyed in my tower, on her bed of silk."

He followed her from the stream, and called out to her: "Maiden."

She turned, startled. There stood a man in a purple robe, tall and stern, with a bloodless face. His eyes were dull yet burning. His eyes were too large. They swallowed up his face, and her.

She followed him over the rough ground. On the cruel hills her feet bled from the stones. The moon came up. A black horse rode with her on his back, mane like jet ribbons, flying fast, leaping the chasms, swimming the cold Wide River.

"Takerna!" Volk cried out, in the tower, "High Lord of Night."

Takerna he conjured, conjured him out of that stone chip hung round his neck, conjured the image up on the floor. There the god stood, as on the mountain, as on the hill above the quarries.

Volk made, as once before, the magic he himself had created, out of thought and desire and grim determination. He laid the maiden of Yevdor at the idol's feet, and slashed her wrist with a pale blade. He understood at last what it was he was giving, had given, what it was the god took. It was the meat from the animal sacrifice, another thing with humans. Not the intelligence of the brain, or the animation of the body, not actually the shadow—for that was the symbol rather than the substance.

Dawn came through the eastern windows, the color of the maiden's hair.

"Get up," Volk said to her. She rose. Her face was white as marble, her eyes were dark as forests. She saw him, or sensed him, and, sensing too the being of the idol in him, she bowed until her tresses swept the floor of the tower. She was as beautiful as a dream and as empty as an unfilled cup.

For Takerna, the black god, had devoured her soul.

Jy's troupe came down the hill road and forded the Wide River of the Volkyan Plain.

Jy was older now, nine years older and more clever, nine years drunker, too, and with pewter streaks in his beard. A new actress rode among the carts, flower-like of face, and sharp as a needle. Six tumblers and jugglers rode

at the back, and a dozen or so assorted actors: here two
arguing, here three lazy ones, trying to have a fight without getting off their ponies, here a boy running along with
an armful of stuff fallen off a cart, there Roshi the fat
man, playing a pipe, sweet as a nightingale.

"Damned rabble," roared Jy affectionately. "Not worth
your keep. Where's that villain Dasyel Parvelson-of-six
bitches and a mule without legs?"

Dasyel begged the actress's pardon—he was riding
beside her, where else?—and came up alongside Jy.

"What does the uncle of misfortune want?"

"Want? Am I supposed to want something before I call,
I, the Prince of the leaders of Troups?"

"The wineskin is to your left," Dasyel said solicitously,
"and the beerskin on the other side."

"Beerskin be worked into certain parts of your anatomy
I am too delicate to mention. Look up yonder, precious
wretch. What do you see?"

"Something shining," said Dasyel. "A tavern, maybe?"

"Impudent pup, your eyesight's as vile as your singing."

"Well then, perhaps an old tower."

"Yes," said Jy, sighing deeply, "so it is. For a minute, I
imagined I saw a roof of gold."

Presently they came upon two peasants traipsing east
along the road towards distant Svatza.

"Ho, you there, what's that place up on the hill?" bellowed Jy.

The peasants muttered.

"Name no names," said one.

"*His* mansion," said the other. "The wolf's lair. The *sorcerer*."

"Oh, some crackpot magician, is it?" thundered Jy, taking perverse pleasure in observing the peasants shudder
and wince. Turning in the cart, Jy directed his great voice
towards the tower, now dull and ruinous in the sunlight.
"Come to the town, old man! Come see the best acting
troup in the Korkeem. Come, turn your whiskers white,
Lord of the Wide River!"

The peasants took to their heels.

To his heels, also, Jy should have taken.

It was market day the next day in Svatza town. Pigs
and goats and carts filled every lane. Soldiers idled, and
the bad, bold women came out on the street and swayed

their hips. Under the river the dungeon still lay like a
black worm: that dungeon that had eaten so many of Kernik's years, while high as a bird in a nest, the governor's
house shone white and rich in the sun. Jy smacked his lips,
foreseeing profit.

One show they did for the people at noon and, sure
enough, to the governor's house they were presently summoned to act in the big stone courtyard there at midnight.

"Goose for dinner," said Jy, "and apples and red wine."

"Maybe only bread and cheese, like the last governor's
house," said the needle actress, "and a cup of *milk*."

"Bah!" said Jy, and Roshi the fat man laughed sympa-
thetically.

Yet it was in fact a good dinner, for the governor had
guests that night—three of his wife's cousins he wished to
impress.

The moon ran up the sky like a silver ball on a thread
of stars. The torches were lit around the sides of the courtyard, while on the slopes of the hill above, where the
house stood, half the town had come crowding to see the
actors again, and buzzed to itself like a hive of bees.

The governor of Svatza was sitting in his carved chair
ready to be entertained, when there came a sudden bang-
ing of doors. Out ran a servant.

"Sir, someone has come."

"Who has come?"

"Someone would not give his name."

"Surely, my dearest," remarked the governor sourly to
his wife, "there is not one of your kin we have forgotten?
No, I thought not. Go and send the man away," he added
to the servant. "Possibly, if we are in the mood, we will
see him tomorrow."

A cold wind blew across the governor's neck. Turning
involuntarily, he glimpsed a tall, dark figure standing in
the open, lighted door. Very tall it was, and narrow. It
nodded to him as only an equal or a superior would dare.

"Forgive my intrusion," said the figure, "we are near
neighbors, but I think we have not met before. I understand there are actors here tonight."

"There are. But I fail to see—" began the governor.

"You understand," said the dark figure, moving forward
so that the red torches fell like snow on a snow-white face
and died in a pair of shineless eyes, "that I received a previous invitation."

"Did you?" asked the governor. His throat felt tight. He recognized a certain description, recalled a certain story, concerning a certain personage who dwelt here and there and often rather near on the Volkyan . . . Could that be a collar of pure gold staring there under the horrid white face? And rubies on those ghastly thin fingers, bloodless and excessively nailed? Dear mercy of the gods—

"Did you require my name?" gently inquired the guest. "My name is—"

"No, no, indeed not. Pray do not speak it. I will have a chair brought—or two? Who is that behind you? No, no—no matter, it's all one—bring two chairs—several chairs!"

The stranger—strange yet not unknown—smiled urbanely. The governor panted out his orders, his wife was pale as a glass of white wine. The three cousins trembled, the servants knees knocked together in chorus. Up on the hill a great quiet had fallen. You might hear the torches spit and sputter at forty paces. Only the actors, waiting for the midnight bell to strike in the town, were blissfully unaware, as yet, that Jy's invitation to the magician had been heard. And answered.

Volk Volkhavaar sat on a chair at the governor's side. Maybe it was pleasant to him to recall that here, shivering and quaking, was the man who by proxy had sent him, so long ago, to Svatza jail. Behind the chair of Volkhavaar stood two of his conjurations in the forms of two servants in black, with hooded faces and gloved hands. At his side sat a maiden dressed in white and silver, with a net of sapphires over her yellow hair. Like a statue she sat, her eyes fixed before her.

"My daughter. I call her Yevdora," said the magician.

The governor, still in terror of names, feigned not to hear.

Just then the bell sounded from all the temple towers of Svatza.

Out strode Jy, on to the rostrum at the center of the paved court. He bowed to the four corners and rapped on the ground with his staff of peeled wood. Full of food and wine and with pewter streaks in his beard, he took that great silence for interest, and did not note the dark figure at the governor's side.

Out came the prologue, glittering with glass gems; Roshi, a fat, yellow sun in a sun-mask.

Tonight it was to be a play for aristocrats to watch, concerning gods and shepherds; it was the humble villages that clamored for princesses and emperors.

The silver lady of the moon, deserting her husband the sun god, favored a simple herdsman on the hills and presently conceived a child by him. This child, brought forth in a cave and left among his father's people, soon grew up into a heroic young man, half peasant and half deity. The sun, furious at this proof of his shame, sent darkness to cover the earth. Our hero left to seek him over the cloud mountains and the circus-roads of the sky. Intrigues were thwarted, monsters slain, and a star maiden won to wife, before the shepherd-hero gained his stepfather's forgiveness, and the world was released from the grip of night.

Every glittering appurtenance was put into action for this play. The moon lady descended from the upper air by means of silver ropes, fireworks were let off to complement the sun's rages, and powder thrown on the torch flames to produce a livid violet glare during the eclipse. Dasyel, in the person of the shepherd-hero, exchanged his fleeces and rags for fantastic star-armor given him by the star-maiden, and closed with multi-colored monsters, containing three or even four actors, and with red smoke issuing from the jaws. A deadly poison, knocked to the ground, appeared to metamorphose into a rat.

The crowd in the court and the crowd on the hill were swept up by the play and its effects to such an extent that they half forgot the dark menace in their midst. As ever, the gasps came and the cries went up and the cheers. Women stared at Dasyel, and the governor eyed the flower-faced star-maiden hungrily, wondering if . . . ? When Roshi stamped and four gold rockets shot from his shoulders, the governor's wife gave a small scream and then pretended she had not, and looked round haughtily to see who had.

So magic met magic, the dark with the bright.

Volk Volkhavaar was watching too, taking everything in as he had always done.

In him there came a stirring, faint, profound. He saw a power, gaudy and transparent though it might be, rivalling his own. He saw how the people lost sight of his terror in the voyeuristic terrors and joys of the rostrum. He looked at Jy, the showman with the staff, at the young actor with

the curling black hair and the looks that made every
woman a pair of round eyes and a beating heart. Maybe a
little jealousy nibbled the nerves of Volk, he who had
never been fair and loved, only pitied, feared and hated.
Maybe. Whatever else, he saw the new joke ready at hand,
waiting like a glove for him to put on.

Presently Roshi, the sun, forgave Dasyel, the hero, and
his silver mother. The torches flashed red again and the
rostrum, yellow. Amid vast, rejoicing, drums, strings and
pipes, the hero and the maiden were wedded and firework
stars cascaded from the sky.

The crowd on the hill was roaring, the governor smiling
and sending for purses, the actors bowing and modestly
waving the applause away from themselves to each other,
when Volk Volkhavaar rose from his chair and went forward like a straight, black smoke, across the courtyard,
right on to the rostrum.

He came up where Dasyel stood with the actress, near
enough to see the mending in the sky armor and the starry
dress, the black actors' paint round both their eyes, the
young and flawless skin of both, smooth as metal and
brown from the road. Volk smiled at the actress and she
took half a step in retreat. Volk looked harder at Dasyel;
Dasyel did nothing, only looked back at him with his
water-color eyes, unflinching, confident, open. And Volk
felt that same passage of non-sexual yet demanding lust go
through him as he had felt when he saw the maiden from
Yevdor.

Then he turned and looked for Jy.

Jy stood with his staff at the far end of the rostrum. He
had finally ascertained that all was not well with the world
in Svatza. That damned silence had come down again
where it had no business to be, and the governor looked
like he might be wetting his elegant drawers. Who was this
gruesome stranger? Jy faced him.

"You're welcome, sir. I am Jy, leader of the troupe.
Have you a complaint? Or are you in a giving, generous
vein? The roads, I may say, are hard, and any gift of
yours—"

"I am thinking," said Volk Volkhavaar, "that you are
something of a magician, Master Jy."

Jy laughed.

"I? Oh, no doubt, no doubt. Jy, the Clever Showman.
Jy, the Prince of Conjurors, I have been called that too.

Master of Acrobats and Actors, High Priest of Entertainment, Lord of the Laugh. Don't think I boast. Ask anyone."

"And here is your sorcerer's wand," said Volk Volkhavaar, setting his hand lightly on the leader's staff. "Do you suppose, if you were to loan it to me, I might make magic too?"

Jy glanced down and saw that loathsome bloodless hand with its long sable talons, furled like a venomous insect round the staff.

"Take it, sir, by all means," said Jy, letting go reflexively.

Volkhavaar took the staff. He rapped on the ground with it. He called out a word or name that no one knew: Takerna.

At once the flames of all the torches turned black, giving off, impossibly, a brilliant, dark light that made every face like the face of a drowned corpse.

A convulsive shudder went over the crowd, but no one ran away. No one dared.

"How's that?" asked Volk. "Not bad for a beginner."

He rapped with the staff again. Rays shot from it, the color of blood. Wherever a ray struck a fantastic animal appeared, animals of six legs or eight, three heads or four, with tails like whips and eyes like larva.

Volk laughed, not as Jy had laughed. He snapped his fingers and his nails smote each other.

Above, the sky turned blindly pale, and a huge, black swan came flying with a fiery beak. The shadow of its wings covered the courtyard, the mansion, the hill. There was a great yelling and hiding of heads. It passed close and bore northwards, a bird as big as four horses, its feathers smelling of smoke and night.

Volk turned about. He gestured over the actors as if giving them his blessing. The actress wore a dress of flames. She shrieked and tried to beat them out. Dasyel caught her wrist. The bright, tin sword in his hand had turned to a serpent that writhed and spat at him, but he held it grimly. Fat Roshi stood transfixed, a big, blond bear on its hind legs.

"Well now," said Volk Volkhavaar, bowing low to Jy, "tell me honestly, what do you think? Don't be kind now, don't try to coddle my feelings."

Jy found a voice.

"Your talents, sir," he said hoarsely, "are—immense. They defy praise."

"Spare my blushes," said Volk. He snapped Jy's staff in two and threw both sections in the air. One piece became a worm, the other a toad. The toad opened its mouth, swallowed the worm, and back into Volk's grasp fell the whole staff in one piece.

Volk snapped his fingers a second time. The torchlight changed from black to red, the sky grew dark, the stars reappeared. All the monstrous things vanished, and Roshi was a man again.

Volk glanced at the young actor. Not so confident now, those son-of-a-rich-man's eyes, and not so open.

Volkhavaar stepped down from the rostrum. He began to walk back to the line of chairs. The governor's wife had fainted and not even the three cousins had troubled to revive her.

The fair-haired maiden rose from her place, and Volk's two 'servants' followed her.

"Er, pardon me, illustrious sir."

Volk halted. He turned about, he bowed.

"At your service, Master Jy."

"My staff," said Jy, his voice coming more strongly. "I think you still have it."

All those years of wine shops had finally told on Jy. He had made the fatal mistake of his career.

"Are you quite certain, Master Jy, that you wish to take back your staff?"

Jy perhaps saw his error then, but it was too late.

"Unless you have a particular use for it, exceptional sir. In which case, of course—"

"Not at all," said Volkhavaar. "You want your property, then I shall give it you."

It seemed he flung the staff, or did it take wing? Midway in its flight it ceased to be either a staff or wood. It became a sword of fine-forged iron, its point like a thin, hard wire. It plunged into Jy's breast with such force that the slim point reemerged from between his shoulder blades. The blow sent him staggering but did not quite fell him. Then he looked down, touched at the quivering hilt, and crashed heavily backwards on the cold stones of the courtyard.

"Where is that damned boy?" muttered Jy.

"Here he is, uncle," said Dasyel.

"Is it the cloak you've put under my head? Stupid mule of a bitch's son, the silver cloth will get dirty on the ground. Do you know nothing?"

"Jy, listen to me," said Dasyel. "That was no sword struck you, but the staff. There's no blood. An illusion only. Now shake yourself and get up."

"Never shout challenges after magicians," said Jy sleepily, morosely. "Not a sword you say, you wretch? Who cares where the wind blows from, south or north, if it blows hard enough, it will have the apples down. I'm for the belly of the Mother. No more taverns for me." Then he grunted. "Who's that throwing water on my face? Eh? Speak up, you devils. Is someone crying?"

"It's rain," said Dasyel.

Jy's two eyes narrowed, peering at him.

"An actor's business is lies," he said, "so why can't you lie decently, you young fool?" Then he caught his breath once, and let it go forever.

Dasyel stood up. The tears ran freely down his face, taking the black actor's paint with them. He was not the only one weeping among Jy's troup.

The governor's wife had come to, and was having hysterics. The three cousins and the governor were arguing fiercely. The crowd on the hill slope was flying homewards as if from a sudden storm.

Of Volk Volkhavaar and his companions there was no longer sight nor sign.

"Dasyel," said the actress, her voice blunted by salt water, "don't think of going after him. He is all they say, that one."

"So much is evident," said Dasyel. "Don't suppose I think I can fight magicians." But somewhere inside him a host of ancestors were howling for vengeance, blood for blood, that inexorable tradition among all noble families, east, west, south or north on the Korkeem. However much good sense and wise cowardice your brain spoke to you, there were always the passionate demons of your heart who could speak louder.

* 10 *

There was a funeral in Svatza town, Jy's funeral. The
actresses sold gold beads and painted brooches given them
by city admirers, the actors sold best boots, saddlecloths
and rings from similar sources. Svatza wanted to ignore
the burying, out of fear of the magician. The actors would
not let it. Jy went into his grave with somber splendor.
When the priest mumbled the words, Dasyel stepped up,
silenced him, and spoke impromptu the melodic valedic-
tion from some play, ringing clear, in a voice half bronze,
half silver.

Westward in his tower, Volkhavaar waited.

He waited for Dasyel to come after him.

When Dasyel did not come, Volkhavaar grinned, between anger and amusement. So young and aristocratic,
that noble actor, so cool and clever.

Spiders spin webs. Volk too.

That night the actors held their wake about Jy's grave.
There were cakes and red wine and lamps burning. Jy lay
below in his best clothes, a gold coin on one eye, a silver
coin on the other, his moustaches and his beard exactly
combed. No one must weep at a wake, or the spirit would
get up and chide you, and no one could be merrier or wild-
er than actors when they put their minds to it.

Then, near midnight, between the mounds of the graves,
a slender shape came stealing. It stole towards the noise of
the wake, and presently, finding Roshi the big man, red-
eyed and tippling under a tree, murmured very low to
him:

"Is Dasyel with you? I must speak to him, for my life, I
must."

Roshi looked up and saw a lovely girl's face gazing at
him from under a hood. Death was hard, but what better
to cheer Dasyel than such a one?

"Wait there, pretty. I'll fetch him." Roshi winked sadly
and went off.

89

Dasyel was drunk. He had felt it needful to be so. When Roshi whispered in his ear, Dasyel rose and came after him. As matters stood, a woman was the last thing he wanted that night, but the wine spoke to him, perhaps, the way wine generally may be relied on to do.

Roshi, being a good sort, and besides, having other melancholy fish to fry, left Dasyel alone beneath the graveyard trees where the cloaked girl was waiting.

"Good evening," said Dasyel bowing. "I am honored to make the young lady's acquaintance."

Then the girl pushed away from the hood and came forward where the light could find her and he saw who it was, even to the sapphires in her golden hair. The companion of the magician.

"Oh, Dasyel," she said softly, "Dasyel."

"You are a long way from home, madam," said Dasyel, sobering faster than was comfortable. "Maybe you should be going back there."

"Dasyel, listen to what I have to say before you judge me. Do you suppose my master's crimes are mine? Do you suppose I went with him gladly to the governor's house or watched him treat you so, with joy? Do you think I laughed and clapped my hands when he killed your leader? No, Dasyel, I wept, but in my heart, not from my eyes. I would not dare weep openly before him." Then she raised those eyes to Dasyel's face, dark eyes brimming with tears indeed. "Look at me. Do you think me happy? He dresses me in fine clothes with gems for my hair, but he stole me from my father's house where I was glad and innocent. Never a kind or a good word does he speak to me. I am less than his cat, which he likes well enough. If ever I displease him, I am punished." Then the maiden came up close to Dasyel. She unbuttoned her silken sleeve and there on the white skin of her arm was a terrible mark as if she had been burnt. "When we were in the tower," she said, "he spoke of your leader's death, boasting, laughing at what he had done. I could not hide my thoughts from him, so he took a brand from the fire, and this he did with it."

The wine had turned to vinegar.

"Lady, have you never tried to leave him?"

Yevdora lowered her eyes and buttoned her sleeve.

"You saw his power. Do you suppose I should escape far? Who would shelter me? Who would dare?"

"Tomorrow," said Dasyel, "we travel south. Come with us."

"You risk too much," said she. "He would kill us all."

"He would have to kill me first," said Dasyel, his angry ancestors getting the better of him. The girl was very beautiful, never had he seen a girl so fair. Too many heroes had spoken with his voice; for six years he had been vowing rescue and chivalry before a crowd. Now the play was real. "Don't be afraid," he said to her, and took her cool hand. "You trust me a little or you would never have sought me out."

"Yes, brave Dasyel, sweet and kind Dasyel. I trust you. And there is a way. But only one. You must kill Volk Volkhavaar. I know of the means—only one thing will do it. Once he told me, offered it to me, mocking my fear. There is a certain knife. It lies in a casket of black iron in the red room of the tower. He uses it to offer to his god, the Dark One, Takerna. This knife loves the taste of blood, and if it could, would have his. By his spells he can master it, but when he sleeps. . . . If you take that knife, and go to his bedside and plunge it into him, no sorcery on this earth can save him." Yevdora stared up once more into Dasyel's face. "Brave lord, are you brave enough for that?"

Dasyel had sobered, but not entirely. The old dreams for vengeance were clamoring, and the girl's loveliness bewitching him and the words of all the heroes in whose armor he had ever clad himself. For a man can be one thing when he is himself, but when his past and his dreams get hold of him, then there is another man altogether.

"Young lady," he said, "you had better stay here till I return. Tell me where this red room is, and where your master sleeps."

"No," she said. "I am no warrior, but neither will I leave all the work to you. I have brought with me one of the magician's horses. It runs more swiftly than any other steed, even with two on its back. Come, I will show you."

Dasyel glanced between the boughs of the tree. The firelight and the wake were still going on, and Jy still lying quiet under the silver coin and the gold. Dasyel turned and went after Yevdora, between the graves, and presently, in the cold light of the moon, they found the horse. Dasyel mounted, the girl sat behind him and wrapped her slim arms about his waist.

At a touch of the reins, the horse leapt forward on to the black highways of the night.

Truly, the horse went swiftly. Its hooves ate up ground, of which rough and smooth seemed all one.

The actors had travelled more slowly with their carts and ponies; it had taken them most of a day to cross the distance from the tower by Wide River to the gate of Svatza town.

The horse swam the river. The cold water lashed Dasyel's legs to his thighs. It was like the teeth of Death himself.

The moon was down, only the stars burned, and the air on the hills was charged with that blank silence which fills the last hours of the night.

The tower, when they came up under it, looked dark, ruinous and old. There was an arched doorway, empty of a door, through which the girl led him after they had left the horse. A courtyard lay beyond with forty steps going up from it to a narrow entrance in the wall.

Dasyel looked up that stair. His blood seemed to freeze for no specific reason. 'Well, you are here,' he said to himself. 'Act out the part now, you have cast yourself in it, Dasyel Parvelson.' Yet he felt his death, cold and close as the jaws of the river had been. Useless to make light of it or plan evasion. He glanced down at the girl. She had murmured in his ear as they rode, near as a lover, told him that at the stair's head lay the red room and the knife in the iron box, that just beyond the curtain there Volkhavaar lay sleeping.

And he had believed all this. Suddenly it seemed to him that only an idiot or a child would have believed a word. But too late now to turn away, for some heavy, cruel hand seemed on his back, moving him towards the stair. One foot on the first step, second foot on the second step, first foot on the third step—Dasyel's head swam but somehow he did not miss his footing.

Then there was the narrow doorway. The door opened. There was a red room, red silk on the walls, red candles burning with clear red flames, red flags on the floor, red glass dark as fever in the window.

And here, in a chair forged from red copper, sat Volk Volkhavaar, an iron knife across his knees, facing him.

"Welcome, sir actor, sir nobleman's son. Pray step over the threshold."

Dasyel found he had done so. And someone had entered behind him—Yevdora. She went by Dasyel as if he were invisible, went to Volkhavaar and stood before him.

"Don't blame the maid," said Volkhavaar," She is my shadow, my only shadow, for see, I cast no other. She does all I tell her to do. Yevdora, turn and face our guest." Yevdora turned. "Yevdora, weep." Yevdora wept. "Yevdora, laugh." Yevdora laughed. "Yevdora, tell the young actor how you love him." Yevdora fell on her knees on the red floor and spoke words of love in a tone trembling with passion. "Yevdora, tell the young actor how you hate him." Yevdora rose. She came to Dasyel. She spoke words of the gutter and spat at his feet. "Yevdora, sleep." Yevdora stood like a statue, her gaze grown blind. "As you see," Volkhavaar said, "she is an excellent actress and most realistic, for she believes whatever instructions I give her."

Dasyel was uncertain, his sight was confused, his brain cloudy; a slow wintry poison was flooding through his veins. He felt no fear, only a distant anger, at the magician, at himself.

"I am thinking," said Volkhavaar, "that I, too, might lead a troup of actors. To Arkev, perhaps. Some quiet noons I hear the picks strike in the quarries of white stone and I recall One who has only a small temple in Arkev, queen-city of the Korkeem. See, I have my staff." He pointed, and Dasyel found he could only look where the magician pointed, and there indeed was a leader's staff of peeled wood with a dark stone set at its tip. "Oh, that," said Volkhavaar, "that is my talisman, part of my lord, Black Takerna."

The lethargy seemed to seep from the magician's eyes. Dasyel tried to speak, but the sentence stuck in his throat.

"You have a strong will, sir actor," said the smiling wolf in his copper chair, "but you have lived soft compared to my living, and my will is stronger. Say farewell to yourself, for presently the High One will have your blue blood. Say farewell to life and love and carefree hope and all your little ambitions. Say it *immediately*. Is it said? I trust it is, for now you go out with the candles."

And like the blow of an icy fist, the magician's power

struck Dasyel between the eyes. And night fell on his heart
and mind as the sun rose over the river.

The actors guessed where Dasyel had gone. They fled
from Svatza, off the Volkyan Plain, all but Roshi.

Roshi struck out for the tower, fat and troublesome to
his pony, sweating and grim. Jy had been most dear to
Roshi, and Dasyel also, for he was Jy's fosterling. And
besides, Roshi recalled the girl in the graveyard, and
blamed himself. He reached the tower, which that day
looked only like rock. At first he could not find it. *Then*
he found it.

Volk Volkhavaar was glad. The fat man with his piper's
skills was a valuable addition to any troup of players.

Presently a black flower was harvested. Kernik, the
Clever Showman and Stealer of Scenes, set out with his
troup—the demon jugglers, the magic birds and goats and
dragons and the fat buffoon, the fair maiden, the handsome actor—and travelling westwards towards Arkev,
came eventually on a village at a mountain's foot, Old
Ash's village; Old Ash, who owned the raven-haired slave
girl, Shaina. . . .

PART THREE

The Soul and Its Flight

* 11 *

A white leaf was blowing over the high night sky of the Korkeem. A white leaf with the stars shining through it.

Shaina's soul.

Up from the little villages, lampless and sleeping she blew, over the soft, blue spheres of the hills, the harsher ridges of mountain slopes clad with trees all gemmed with silver by the setting moon, and in the shadow beyond the moon with forest like the black curls of a young man's hair. Over the grey uplands, the staring peaks, slender as daggers, streams below embroidered flashingly on the dark, over into the sky arching other valleys, other hills, other little villages all bound together in the smoky nets of night. Westward lay the town of Kost. She passed above it. Lights still smouldering there dull red, pale violet in the taverns, and one fallen star on the temple tower, watching her. It went fast, the white leaf soul of Shaina, faster than any bird or any wind of spring. Yet everything she saw, and saw it through the gaze of her love and her dream, beauty made more beautiful.

Once an owl, hunting on the upland airs, veered off from her transparent luminence. She guessed from the slow heavy flight of it how swiftly she was moving.

Soon the towns began to gather, closer and closer to each other. More lights burned below. A river opened like a shining black road across the land. Mansions lay on either side, ivory-pale, and wharfs where ships were slumbering, their sails folded like the wings of doves. One ship travelled beneath her down the wide highway of the river, a white swan with purple torchlight on her prow and spread before her in the water.

The city became apparent gradually. It crept up on the curve of the world and over it, a mountain landscape of towers and polished domes and high roofs of fabulous metal. A thousand lamps yet kindled there making its temples into shells of flame. And here was a palace of white stone with gold moons resting on its pinnacles.

Arkev, sky-worshiping city, mistress of the Korkeem, the Duke's respected home.

Arkev, where one had come, a dark one, smiling, with his troup of actors on black horses. Volkhavaar's city, soon though not quite yet.

Arkev, where someone lay sleeping, or seeming to sleep, for who can say the soulless ever wake? Someone with curling hair that Shaina loved.

There was to be a fair at Arkev in the morning. From far and wide they had been coming, the people of the roads. Actors, peddlers, doctors, merchants. The fair would last for twelve days, to mark the Spring Festival of the Sun. Along the perimeters of the huge market place, the Great Square of Arkev, which spread south to the Duke's palace, north and west to the temples, and east to the marble-paved banks of the river Karga, all the pavilions, the carts, the wagons of a hundred or more groups of itinerants lay scattered and huddled in patchwork, jewel-colored ranks. While up to the bright wharf the boats had snuggled, rubbing their tarry sides lovingly on the stone. Occasional torches fluttered on poles among the alleys of this second, makeshift city of tents and ships. Here, the shoemakers' quarter, needles still busy by candle flicker, here, the apothecaries' corner, cauldrons a-bubble. Birds in cages and sheep in pens, and two or three men late-drinking at a canvas wine booth, and a bearded witch in a green cloth arbour puzzling over a tray of beads.

Northward, the actors' tents, gorgeous as peacocks and with belled banners planted in the ground outside. Was Kernik here? Kernik the High Priest of Entertainment, Kernik with his troup?

Something came drifting down, a fragment of mist, a gauzy scarf, a cloud out of the sky, over the pavilion city. Yet it did not pause above the actors' encampment; it passed over and on to the spot where the square ran upwards into one narrow street that lost itself at its summit in a grove of tall poplars. Beyond the grove a hidden garden, all shadow.

A sanctuary of night the garden was. Night close held under its boughs of oaks and larches, breathing out the murky breath of its ferns and wild flowers the color of slate in the shade. At the garden's center a ruined shrine.

Its door was barely high enough to admit a man, two roughhewn pillars pointed at a broken roof, its walls were overgrown with briar.

Into this place the pale thing came blowing, and floated down on the grass. A young girl's soul stood in the garden, a silver thread drifting away behind it, an invisible thread of love lying before.

Somewhere in Arkev a bell was ringing. It was the hour before dawn.

In the garden it was difficult to be certain, to comprehend for sure how many black pavilions had been put up about the shrine, how many black horses—if any—stood silent and still as basalt in the gloom. Was there a lamp glowing near, or was it star-shine? Did someone speak in the ruin, whispering a prayer, or was it the wind fingering the briars? What matter? Shaina's spirit looked and listened for one sight, one sound.

She passed over the turf, her ghost hair flowed through the leaves like milk. Through a tent wall of sable velvet she passed, straight through, and there she found him.

The hearts of spirits cannot beat, yet it seemed to her they could, for surely hers was beating, or did she hear the beat of his, the heart of Dasyel, beating as he slept?

She hung like a dream above him. Her eyes felt full of tears, though souls cannot weep. She reached to touch his hair, and her hand melted into it and straight through into the pillow under it, and she chided herself for feeling such absurd sorrow that she could not, after all, touch him.

He was more beautiful, she thought, than she had recollected, and yet he seemed known, familiar to her as someone she had seen every day for a year. Yet was he not pale? Thinner also? Vulnerable with sleep, he lay before her like her child, shadows like smoke beneath his eyes.

Shaina's soul faltered then in its longing, speechless, staring. What now? What must be done? She wanted to kiss his mouth, wake him up, say to him: Here I am. Surely you know me? Or perhaps his soul, drifting to consciousness even as he lay insensible, would reply to her voiceless importuning. What would that soul of his say, roused like a dark angel out of oblivion? Perhaps: You are nothing to me. Go home and be damned, I have no time for you. Yes, the soul of Shaina was capable of humility, shame and shyness. It lingered by him, wondering, thinking of Barbayat's words: "Soul calls to soul, and soul

answers. When you find him can you doubt his soul will
wake to the yearning in yours? How can he fail to love
you also? Love does not come as your love came unless
there is already a bond between the two of you, and if he
is blind to it now, his spirit will see with different eyes."

'Oh, Dasyel,' thought Shaina then, 'did she only lie to
me to exact her price? They say the promise of a witch is
like a plain woman, seldom remembered. Oh, Daysel.'

Dasyel lay still as death and good to look on as the sky,
and the bright flame in Shaina's heart went out, leaving all
dead and dim behind it. 'Well, I will be going then.' But
still she hovered there, imagining that yet there must be
some way to tell him of her presence and her love, if only
she could learn of it.

Eventually there came a little anger. Her head went up,
her soul's head, in the old gesture of pride under duress:
Maybe then, you do not want me. I'm sorry to have troubled you. This cleared the dream from her a little, like a
harsh brush bringing down cobwebs, and at once, for the
first time, she felt the danger all about her.

She had been confusing it all along with the shadows
themselves, this oppression, this sense of something
watching. Easy to do so, for it was like the night—black,
omnipresent and absolute. Now her very spirit shrank.
How chill the tent was, how graveyard cold the garden.
Two impulses came then, hand in hand. One told her to
stay, she *must* stay, there by the sleeping lover who refused to know her. She had not forgotten the vision the
witch gave her, true or false, of the iron wheel and Dasyel
bound on it, sleeping forever. The second impulse, however, was stronger. It spoke of flight: The young man casts
no shadow, he is part of this wickedness, at home with it,
not only the magician's slave, but his foster son.

There was a weird vibrating note that twanged in the
core of Shaina like a discord of strings—it was the silver
chain which bound her to her own flesh, seeming to tug at
her, call to her—come back, come back, before it is too
late.

And suddenly she found she could not resist this urge to
save her existence. She was free of the tent before she
even meant to leave it, up in the wide acres of the air. She
did not need breath, yet she gasped: she felt like a minnow
which had escaped the clashing jaws of the pike, a pigeon
that the stooping falcon missed by a feather's breadth. The

slender cord which had unwound from its unguessable
source without tension to let her fly where she wished,
now reeled her in. She was pulled, turning and spinning,
through the high fields of space, noticing nothing but a
wild unreasoning terror. The nature of time was changed.
One moment the stars were glancing like sharp knives
across her face, then came a tumbling through fire, a
smothering well of blindness, after which she lay becalm-
ed, and felt the heaviness of mountains piled on top of
her.

Presently she stirred.

Great weights held down her hands, but somehow she
dragged them upwards, showed them to herself like the
hands of another. She had put on flesh again. She had
reentered her body's envelope. The village of her bondage
enclosed her.

She was as before, save that the night was nearly gone.

The ashes of the fire were grey, the light of the sky grey
also. Outside, the dog was rattling its fetters. Crags stood
against the sky, the birds began to sing in the willows by
the stream. Soon she must rise, she and this leaden thing
hung on her, which was herself.

Had the night been a dream? If so the dream was dead.

She lay immobile. She thought of her fear and her
flight. She thought of the young actor, relaxed in his indifferent slumber. She understood nothing. No longer would
pride sustain her. There had been too high a hill of joy
and hope. She had climbed it singing. Then fallen from
the summit. She lay and wept in silence, as she had long
since learned to do.

Far off, something was happening. This far: many days
and many nights journey away, unless the traveller was a
time-twisting, spell-making magician or a free flying spirit
of a young girl in love. In Arkev, in a garden of trees, an
entity who had once been a man, came from the fallen
shrine of the idol called in those parts, though infre-
quently, Sovan Tovannazit.

Volkhavaar the magician sniffed the fragrant air, and
there was a new scent on it. A scent he recognized. Not of
flowers or grass or dark stone; the perfume of something
living yet incorporeal—a soul. It lay like the dew on the
ground and clung about the sleeping place of the young
actor. Volkhavaar opened the tent flap and there, scattered

over the floor, the couch, the dark hair of Dasyel, lay the faintest of glittering dusts, like dust swept from the palaces of the stars.

The lips of Volkhavaar curled back. He snapped his fingers. The young man opened his eyes, hollow eyes till the magician should fill them with an appearance of sight and animation.

They fastened on Volkhavaar, blind as ice.

"What did you see in the night?" the magician asked of them.

"Blackness," said the lips of Dasvel, "as ever."

Volk laughed then, and Dasyel, being his slave, catching his mood as the empty vessel catches rain, laughed also.

"A moth has been fluttering round my lamp," said the magician. "Come back, moth. Burn your wings next time. The lamp will not trouble."

Having failed, do you accept failure, saying only: Well, it is so. I will turn to other things? When night comes, do you accept the blackness of it, saying only: Well, it is so. I will turn and wait for morning? Or do you go on striving to light a candle against that dark however often the wind blows out the flame, however often the night returns?

To Shaina everything was night. Night in day. Night in the world and in her heart. Hope and love had failed her, or she them. Now no tomorrow beckoned and no bright promise. Only slavery and drudgery remained, and life empty as a desert. Scarcely could she say: I will look for other things, for there were none. Only her mind said sharply: Don't think of him. Time will ease it. And her heart cried in pain.

Even the little food she got in Old Ash's house she did not want. She grew thinner and walked in a different way; there was bitterness in her. No one noticed. Who cared what the slave looked like as long as she did her work?

Besides, the priest they had asked for had arrived from Kost.

He was a portly man, the priest. In his red robes he sat under the shade tree outside Mikli's house, and examined the villagers. He wore the golden symbol of the sun about his neck, and his two front teeth were also gold. Three meals a day were given him, and nothing but the best. Everyone contributed. No one grudged him, they could all see he was working very hard at their problem—the mysterious happenings that had taken place in the valley.

He questioned many people, and thoroughly too, making them repeat their statements. He looked at objects closely, inspected the animals, and once went all round the flocks which the wolf had been troubling, and sprinkled, here and there, little pinches of colored holy dust and spoke strange religious words. The village was gratified. They were in good hands. When they told the tale of the robbers who had stolen the chickens and shut up all and sundry in Mikli's barn, the priest went to investigate the source of the crime. He frowned when he stood there. His clever eyes narrowed. He pulled at his lip, but said nothing. Then:

"Where is Young Ash, the drunken one?" he inquired.

"He has the goats up to pasture," said Gula.

"Then I will see him tomorrow. Now it is dinner time, I think?"

Young Ash—whose six curious bouts of inebriation had caused such alarm—was never drunk now, and for the past eleven days his duties had been fulfilled meticulously. One or two young men over the hill, looking out for him in vain at dusk from the tavern door, had come to the conclusion that he was either in love or dead.

This very sunset, unknowing that there would be an interview with the priest tomorrow, Young Ash, with a bored whistle, was driving the goats back to the village. He past the dark idol cut in the rock, with a bow and a 'good evening', while in the valley Shaina the slave came walking from the well towards Old Ash's house. The priest, as it happened, saw her then for the first time as he was standing under the shade tree. A young girl moving between the reddening shadows, a heavy pitcher in each of her hands.

"Who is that?" asked the sharp priest. "One of your village maidens?"

"No, father," said Mikli, "Old Ash's slave."

"No one mentioned to me that there was a slave here. She must also be spoken to. Nobody must be left out. But now let us go inside to your wife's excellent cooking." Nevertheless, his eyes stayed on Shaina a little while longer as she went up the street, stayed on her princess's gait, and the scrap of linen round her wrist. He had a specialist's nose, had the priest. He had smelled sorcery in Mikli's barn, like old smoke. Now, on the slave girl he smelled a different scent, yet no less strong. He meant to find out what it was, but time enough tomorrow, or the day after; his belly had its interests too, and what a delightful steam was coming from Mikli's cookpot at this very minute. . . .

"Tomorrow, early, the priest wants to see you," snapped Old Ash's wife to Young Ash as he ate his dumplings.

"Why? What have I done now?"

"Hold your tongue and mind your manners and do as you're told, boy! Slave," added the woman, glaring at Shaina, "tomorrow *you* take the goats to grass, and no dawdling."

"Thank you, yes," said Shaina. She was sewing things from a basketfull the wife had given her, and her head drooped for very weariness, not so much of toil but of life itself.

'Shaina, you are a fool,' she thought. It means nothing to take the goats up the mountain. Do not go remembering. Put him from your mind. He is too handsome and too haughty. Next year they will say Dasyel, and you will say: Who is Dasyel? But two tears fell between the stitches of her needle, and each one said: Liar! We shall fall then as now.

The sun rose, cocks crowed, Shaina left her bed by the cold fire, and the dog barked rudely at her.

The goats were glad to see her. She milked them politely and she understood their madness and their jokes, and was more tolerant than Young Ash.

Shaina took a breath of the sweet day. The goats jumping up the bank before her, she began to sing, defiantly, defying herself and her grief and the world which might see it.

Red and gold and white were the flowers in the grass. The sky and the mountains were topaz fading up into sapphire.

"Well, it's not so bad," said Shaina, but she knew it was. Morning, with its intimations of freshness, renewal and exhilaration, was scourge rather than comfort.

Then, coming up the track, she moved around the rock with the carving on it, that image of a demon or a mountain deity. Once, and once only, had she omitted to address this gentleman, that day she had gone to the witch. Never after did she forget, and not today.

"Good morning, sir," said Shaina.

How strange it was, that thing she had noticed earlier, on the evening before the magician came with his actors—how the carving seemed darker, more expressive, *younger*. That bizarre look had faded so that she had thought it only a fancy in the first place, yet today . . . Could it be the dawn light which made that roughhewn face so oddly acute, so malign, and somehow so attentive?

Shaina stopped still, for she noticed that the goats were running, running and leaping to get past the place, as if some devil were really in it. She felt cold, all at once, afraid as she had felt on that night of her soul's flight. But this time she did not fly. The last goat, maa-ing wildly, skittered by and up the slope. Shaina considered the idol. Then, not glancing away from its strange accentuated face, she went right up to it.

There was a shadow on the spot, not the shadow which fell from the rock, rather, something thrown down over her from the clear sky.

"Sir," Shaina said, "what is wrong with you? Have I offended you in some way? If I have, I am most sorry for it."

The idol returned her gaze with its implacable eyes of stone.

"Is it," faltered Shaina, "could it be my *sorrow* which angers you? Or maybe my singing? Pray, don't be cross. My heart is heavy, for which, believe me, I speak to it severely. But like you, sir, I am alone, and likely to continue so, I think." Then Shaina dared to put up her hand, and gently touch the feet of the carving, and on impulse she plucked a white flower growing from one of the cracks in the rock, and laid it over the dark hand which grasped the horn. "See, a sacrifice to appease you, sir. A poor living flower I have killed for you. Be angry no longer. I will try to be happy in this sad land, if you will try to be kind."

After this, a sense of great silliness came over Shaina, as if someone had caught her talking aloud to herself. So she turned directly and ran up the slope after the goats.

And as she ran, it seemed to her she ran towards the very sky itself, and suddenly something burst inside her, like the snapping of a chain.

She rushed into the goats' pasture after the goats.

"Attend to me, goats," cried Shaina, her hands turning

into fists at her sides, her eyes large and bright. "I don't believe I tried hard enough. I don't believe a spell bought with life's blood is to be wasted. I think I should go to him again, and again, despite the place he is in. Twenty times I should go to him, or thirty, or more, until his own soul sits up and tells me to be off. *Then* is the time for crying."

So she made her decision to light once more her candle against the night. Twelve days' sorrow was gone. Burdens had been lifted from her. Everything seemed simple and good, and the promise before her again. Even, it seemed, the demon in the rock might have given her this new will and optimism.

She thrust the clothes into the stream and beat them vigorously. She worked hard and she worked quickly, and all around the goats danced in the pasture.

Afternoon came softly and spread out lazy islands of cloud on the gentian sky, and golden shadows fell over Shaina's face.

She lay in the grass tiredly, among the nibbling herd, and slept. She dreamed of Dasyel in a far city, Dasyel as a king in a jewelled crown, and a black-haired girl beside him in a crown of silver, and she smiled in her sleep.

The sun chariot, drawn by its saffron horses, rose to the last meadow of heaven, and Shaina and the goats came down the mountain. Passing the idol in the rock, Shaina bowed. The image was pale and unmenacing. Warm sunset light revealed only its age, its harmlessness. Gratified, Shaina went on towards the village and, more impatient, towards the night and her hope and her resolve.

She did not see how the white flower, which she had torn up to propitiate the grim god, had taken root again in the barren stone.

* 12 *

Arkev's Spring Fair of the Sun began at dawn, when the priests' chant rose from the Sun Temple. Gongs of gold were beaten, and bursts of pigeons shot into the rose crystal dome of the sky. From the Great City Square came a noise like two armies, four bull-rings, eight orchestras, sixteen taverns. Every color and every sound and scent known in the Korkeem—and a few not known. Wonders opened like flowers and the fans of peacocks, and dusts and incenses spread before the sun chariot in a mauve gauze, as it galloped into the morning.

Southwards of the great market stood the Duke's palace, at the edge of the square. Up rose the enormous outer flight of marble stairways, every twentieth step flanked by two guards in crimson, gold and white, with two white swords in their gold belts, across the last marble landing, under the shadow of the gleaming towers, where the five great entrances blazed in the white walls, each door of hammered bronze inlaid with gold and silver and precious enamels, each door barred by five crimson guards with black wolf-dogs on gold leashes lying around their feet, past all this sparkle and splendor, into the cool blue and white rooms beyond.

Here also, impudently, the noise of the Spring Fair came clamoring, not turned back by stairs or guards or doors or dogs, rattling the stained glass in the windows, waking up the Duke's wife in her satin bed and the Duke's poor plain daughter in her lonely one; not, however, waking the Duke who, beneath a storm cloud of velvet canopy, dreamed of hunting a white, naked, delicate, desirable lemon-haired sprite through the green colonnades of the wood, and catching her by the stream, and—

"Come, now," said the Duke, "I am sure this can be arranged in an amicable manner."

"Maybe not," said the sprite archly. "Generally I slay

107

all travellers who follow me. I lead them into the water and drown them."

"Tut," said the gentleman, putting on a fine air, "I am Moyko, your Duke."

"Indeed, you would be surprised at all the important personages I have had the privilege of drowning, here in my humble stream. In fact, there is only one man I respect and fear too much to treat in this fashion."

"And who is that?" demanded Duke Moyko haughtily.

"Why, Volk Volkhavaar, the Lord of Magicians. Even you, Duke, in your bed of velvet, will doff your cap to *him* when he bids you."

At this the Duke awoke, although it seemed to him that it had been rather a waking than a sleeping dream. He shook himself peevishly and tugged the golden braid by his bed for the servants to bring his morning drink of wine honey and cloves.

"Volk Volk—whatever," he grumbled. "What a thought for the Duke to be having."

Outside the mazarine window glass something flapped its wings and flew off into the sky. A pigeon, perhaps, from the Temple—though it had looked too large, and its beak cruel as a hook . . . falcon, maybe.

Presently, drink drunk and silk clothes donned, rings on his fingers and a collar of rubies around his neck, the Duke lumbered down the bright inner stairways of his palace to breakfast. Fifty years the Duke had amassed, fifty years of getting his own way, thinking his own thoughts; fifty years of knowing the gods beamed on him. When a prince, in his father's time, there had been a few restrictions, though not many. But for ten years now, since that father's death, no restrictions at all. Naturally, he respected his father's memory. The Old Duke, Moyko called him, the corners of his mouth turning solemnly earthwards, his eyes moist. What dead father could ever have had a more loving son. Look at the tomb he had built for him—what a time he had had, too, getting the people of rich Arkev to pay up the extra tax needed to finance it! But the present Duke was a great one for building things. Observe the gold pinnacles on the Temple of the Sun, the silver windows eastward in the Temple of the Moon; just take a glance at the three towers added to the palace. *Oh*, yes. This was a Duke to be reckoned with.

Into the hall he went, fifty years of calcified ignorance,

conceit and silliness, and sat down with a fat, heavy thud before his gemmed plate and took up a gemmed knife.

The Duchess raised her pale-green livid face, and up swam her fishy, spiteful eyes.

"You are late, my Beloved Husband," said she, putting into this traditional term of affection as much dislike and contempt as she could muster.

"I have been thinking," fallaciously said the Duke. "Yes. Hmm. About your daughter's marriage."

The Duke's plain daughter, Woana by name, lowered her lids and blushed a sad, sour puce. No one would marry her, unless she went to the marriage thickly veiled, with seventeen muleloads of dowery hurrying close behind, and this, unhappy girl, she knew. Had she been a poor man's child, she would long since have become a priestess in the Temple of the Moon, hidden herself in its cloisters and been glad to do so. But Princess Woana was not allowed this luxury. Since she had no son, and no prospect now of having one legally, Moyko was bound to secure the future succession in Arkev via his daughter and some trustworthy, virile but not-too-clever young man of the aristocracy. It was a great nuisance, Moyko thought, that the wretched girl had taken all after her mother in the matter of looks, and grown up so unprepossessing. His wife thought much the same, in reverse. Neither claimed her. It was always '*Your* daughter.'

Woana's humiliated, lowered gaze came to rest on the area of mosaic floor by her feet, where her silk-black cat sat licking up cream from a silver dish.

The plain princess had never allowed herself to love another human, rejection being so predictable, but this one thing she did love, her cat, Mitz. Mitz was pretty and graceful, merry, mad, daring and confident, all those things Woana was not. Mitz also had lovers, sleek, furry lovers who sang to her and fought over her, ecstatically ravished and presently left her, with kittens. In a fashion Woana lived through Mitz, all the more so since Mitz remained utterly faithful to her. Only on the princess's swansdown pillows would Mitz sleep, or in the princess's brocade lap. Only from Woana's thin little ringed hand would Mitz accept her food. Only when Woana's throaty, immature, little-girl's voice called her name would Mitz answer. When others stroked Mitz, Mitz yawned and stalked away; when Woana stroked her, Mitz purred, look-

ing up into Woana's face with her triangular pussy countenance and pleasure-slitted emerald eyes. "Meow," said
Mitz, but to Woana this was translated as: Mother, sister,
beloved, best.

"Well," grated the Duchess of the Korkeem, "oh, most
excellent husband. What scheme have you to get your
daughter wed?"

"There is a lord," said the Duke, improvising as he
scooped up ducks' eggs greedily, "Volk something, I forget, from a Plain somewhere—I shall have to give it seri-
ous consideration. *Your* daughter, madam, is getting well
past the age for marriage."

"Nonsense. *Your* daughter is only—let me see—how old
are you, Woana? Oh, never mind, I don't expect she
remembers either. In any case I am heartily sick, indeed I
am, of all this bickering. You recall, I suppose, how bad it
is, the physician said, for my *liver*."

"Meow," said Mitz. She leapt lightly into Woana's arms.
She almost seemed to wink: I am very partial to a little
minced liver.

* 13 *

The actors had come to Arkev from every road that crossed the Korkeem. They had set up their gaudy tents and their banners, and, going through the streets in procession, along the river banks, across the Great Square, they had displayed, like other traders, their exotic wares. Songs, strings, bells and drums, red cloth and yellow, magenta plumes and gilded masks, pretty girls with flowers in their hair and bodices sewn with seed pearls, tricky men producing green snakes from their ears, swallowing fire, walking over up-pointing knives, finding sparrows in their hats. Every day little plays, put on apparently at random, in response to the cheers and demands of the crowd; heroes, villains, gods and terrifying beasts, the stuff of legends, spiced by several vulgar jokes and the eternal heart-clutch of love. Now and then a fight between rival troups, young actors comandeering the tables of taverns, brawling elegantly as foxes, a put-up job, maybe, but who cared? Now and then a fight in earnest—someone stealing someone's props, horse dung mixed into beard glue, breeches sewn together at strategic points. A couple of girls looking daggers because each was said to be the fairer. All of it an art in itself, which was expected of them, a preliminary.

Northwest from the Great Square stood the Temple of the Sun with its walls of glittering brass and its scalding roof of gold with golden domes like curving flames perched there. In the huge open court before it, on a high burnished stage like an altar to the god, the Actors' Festival would begin on the tenth day of the Spring Fair, and continue, sunrise to midnight, for three days more.

The plays ran like a string of beads, one after another. Galvanizing effects were put into each, every troup determined to make every other troup look like the provincial ninnies anyone with discernment could see they were, anyway, could they not? Splendor piled on splendor. The air

111

flashed and winced with the sparkle of facetted glass, reeked with rare incenses and saltpeter.

Two years back, Jy's troupe had played at Arkev's Spring Fair, and won first prize, awarded, as usual, by popular vote of the crowd. The prize was a generous bag of gold, but, true to the tenets of their profession, this bounty was quickly eaten, drunk and otherwise hastily dispatched by Jy and his actors, leaving no mark of its passage. The kudos, however, had remained. The crowds in Arkev were neither tolerant nor partial. You had to win them; if not, decaying cabbages had been known to fly through the air.

This year Jy's name was nowhere to be discovered on the lists which the recorders had made. Indeed, only in Svatza could that name be found, in the graveyard there.

Unknowing and uncaring, meanwhile, the Duke perused the play-lists with his bulbous eye, choosing those he would honor with his presence. He liked the plays; being seen at them, more than seeing them, perhaps. He liked the look of his prosperous city, for whose wealth he gave himself complete credit where little was due. He liked to sit under the brocaded awning on his golden chair, to smile graciously when the performance pleased him, to talk ostentatiously to his underlings when he was not pleased. He liked the way people bowed to him like a field of wheat in the wind.

Seldom did his wife accompany him—her liver would keep her at home, or some other complaint, of which she had a variety, a veritable wardrobe full, so it appeared to him. Every morning, presumably, she stood before this wardrobe, considering, wondering to herself: Shall I put on the headache today, or the chest cold? Or maybe I would look best in my neuralgia.

Woana, however, always came to the plays, and stared at every scene, enthralled as a child. The Duke had frequently rebuked her for this unseemly show of interest, but it did no good; and the nasty cat was always there in her lap, seeming to watch too, and purring. Left to herself, the stupid girl would no doubt have sat through all three days worth and given *everyone* a prize, including the crowd.

On the tenth day of the fair, in the black night-morning before dawn and before the Festival of the Actors began, this happened: stars fell into the streets of Arkev.

Thick and fast they fell. Many saw them. Priests in the towers of shrines, maidens offering in the Moon Temple, watchmen in a hundred doorways and on the decks of fifty ships. Dogs saw them fall and set up a howling which woke half the sleep-buried citizens who, feeling their way to the windows, also saw. Lovers in the midst of love saw them and lost the thread of their discourse; drunkards lying in gutters saw them and reviled the wine they had swallowed. Even the Duke's daughter, creeping to a colored pane, saw the strange stars come, though the Duke did not, for he was busy dreaming.

Silver they were, very bright, yet burning oddly, burning darkly. They settled on Arkev, on roofs, on towers, on paving and in the River Karga. They had all the shape of stars with their jagged icicle points, but additionally, they sang. Their song was this: Kernik is coming, Kernik Prince of Conjurors, Kernik Stealer of Scenes. Let the city be ready for the play to end all plays, and the show to stop all shows.

Especially in the actors' place of tents they fell. Men were stirring here, preparing for the dawn and the sixteen odd dramas to be put on that day. And they heard the stars sing differently. 'Beware,' said the stars, 'Kernik is coming, Kernik and his troup. The troup of Kernik will outshine you all; be ashamed, you rabble. Pack up your carts and go home.' And the stars laughed and went out, as, all over the city of Arkev they were going out, and the lamps being lit in wonder and alarm.

The actors were superstitious. Their eyes narrowed or widened. They called privately on the gods of their various homes, spat, and made ritualistic gestures to avert disaster. But it was a bad beginning, there was not one that did not feel it. And when the sun rose somberly and the Duke came late, yawned and talked through almost every speech, and tin swords bent, rockets failed to explode, lines were forgotten and cues missed, no one was greatly surprised. Someone, something, had put a blight on the actors.

But who was Kernik? His name was on none of the lists the recorders had made, and bands of young men, searching the actors' camp angrily, could not discover him or any of his people.

That night, after the ill-starred day, burning flames fell over Arkev. 'Look for Kernik,' they sang, falling into courts, into pools, past windows and startled eyes, 'Kernik the Master of Dreams and Mysteries.'

In the actors' quarter some had been waiting, knives in their belts. Roses scattered down, blazing like crimson sparks from some huge bonfire up in the air, scattered and coalesced and became one tall flickering shape, a demon walking in the alleys between the tents. It laughed as it passed, a histrionic laugh, entirely suitable considering the area of its manifestation. Some ran out and struck at it—their blades and fists made no impression; it walked through them like a garnet ghost—still laughing, nodding. "Dust, mud, dung," sang the thing. "Why not go back to your dust-heaps, mud-holes, dung-hills?"

The next day some packed up and left. Actors flying omens. Eighteen plays that day. Eighteen plays poorly done. Kernik had cast a spell. The actors cursed him, and ran from the rotten fruit that showered like hail upon the stage.

"Where's Kernik?" yelled the crowd, laughing now also, for word had got around; beginning to grasp the joke, entering into the wicked spirit of it. Kernik's bag of tricks had been so far promising, but anyone who dared such boasting would have to be good, indeed he would. Either they would make a god of him then or, if he proved unsatisfactory, they would get their fun driving him and his troupe from the city like cattle to the butchers. "Come on, Kernik Clever Boots. Come, show us!"

In all the city, Duke Moyko alone was uninterested in Kernik. It was another name which troubled him. His dreams were haunted by devils who threatened to rend him, wild animals who threatened to eat him, lightnings which struck and misfortunes which fell; and when he protested, as in these dreams he always did, that he was their Duke, they answered: "Only one man do we fear: Volk Volkhavaar, the Lord of Magicians. Even you, Duke, in your bed of velvet, will doff your cap to *him* when he bids you."

The third night, the night before the last day of the Actors' Festival, the twelfth and last night of the Fair, Arkev waited up to see what would burst from the sky. No one was disappointed. A thousand swans with sequinned feathers came from the east, the west, the south, the north, and sailed together in an argent swarm above Duke Moyko's own palace. "Kernik," they sang, in the voices of maidens. "Tomorrow, the stroke of midnight." And vanished.

Not so many dared put on their plays that twelfth day. Those that did got little recognition. Everyone was waiting now, even the acting troups waited morosely. To see the great impressario, the Stealer of Scenes. Torches were lit in the blue dusk, and a crescent moon rose, and the crowd had gathered already about the high stage in the Sun Temple court.

Shaina was waiting too, lying waiting in Old Ash's house, that twelfth day of Arkev Fair, which to her was the twelfth day of her sorrow, the day she had come to her senses and decided heartbreak was not yet.

She was afraid of all kinds of things, afraid of her own reckless impatience to begin the journey so early, afraid that the house would never settle to sleep, for Old Ash and Old Ash's wife and Young Ash had been bickering and grumbling all evening about what the priest from Kost had said, and the tavern. Even now they were in bed, she was tensed for some great torrent of shouting to start up once more. Afraid she was, too, that she had forgotten the soul-spell or some vital part of it. More than anything, at last, she was afraid again of the dark place and the danger that surrounded shadowless Dasyel.

Yet quiet came, and faint snores above. Quiet settled over everything but Shaina. She quickened to be off, up into the clear night under the moon.

She began the spell. She had not forgotten it; had forgotten nothing.

The pain came as before, grim and frightful. And, rising out of it, weightless and silver in the air, the surprise, the sense of bliss and freedom, as before, filled her with their spiritual passions.

Until, suddenly, something checked her, made her glance back a second time at the spot where she lay, her own fleshly self, stretched mute and unbreathing by the burned-out hearth.

Shaina's body, a beautiful young girl; skin a transparent honey from the sun, lashes like long black reeds, hair like a night river running under and in rivulets over her maiden's apple breasts, her slim, strong, calloused hands. Her soul looked at it with the old pang of disembodied love, and she thought, as before she had not: Supposing they wake and come down and find me? Will they notice how I am—empty?

But it was too late. She did not care. The scents of starlight trees and hills were luring her like a vixen into the night. Up she swirled, silver Shaina, with her spilling milk ghost-hair, by the disapproving demons, into the ether.

Over the hills, the mountains, the forests, the river, the whole wide almost-midnight land, to Arkev. Flying out of time.

A year later, and a second later, she crested the Star Temple, herself like a star, and was dimmed by the broad glare of a torchlit place away to the north. Arkev, the always-bright. Yet this midnight, every flame seemed settled in that one place, and such a crowd. Down Shaina flew, dissolved in the light, invisible, and wafted like a breath on to the lowest golden lintel of the Temple of the Sun.

Everywhere the crowd was spreading, restless but rooted as a meadow of wild flowers. All through the vast court, and beyond it, every wall and roof and balcony and upper window filled, even the makeshift platforms tottering, men and women gripping there like tame birds gathering to be fed. Nearer, directly below, a rich canopy and a puffy, important man with a golden hat stuck with jewels sitting under it, and soldiers in red and black and white, and two women, one all pale, liverish silk, and the other with a sad little bent-forward head of thin lusterless hair, a small animal bolt upright in her lap. The Duke, the Duchess, and the Princess Woana.

Shaina had paused on the lintel, knowing. She had seen the high stage, she had sensed the excitement, so much greater and more intense, yet so very like the street of Old Ash's village that night when the white-faced man had come there, clacked his claws, and a dragon had rushed from heaven.

The hearts of souls do not beat, their mouths do not grow dry and their bellies do not flutter as if bees and swifts darted about in them. Nevertheless, it may seem to them that all this happens, just as it did to Shaina.

At that moment the midnight bell began to chime.

The crowd, rustling and rumbling before, fell abruptly silent as a tomb. Not a foot stirred, not a word was uttered.

And then—

"Look!" A voice cried, and others: "Look! Look!"

On the stage something had happened, something had appeared. There had been no prologue, no clue given. First the stage was empty; then a figure was occupying it, occupying in the fullest sense.

Seven feet tall it was, or seemed to be, clad in robes of purple nimbus. A crowd of yellow lightnings cracked and sizzled on its head, white scintillas burst from its hands, and when it rapped with its pealed showman's staff, scarlet scintillas.

The midnight chimes were done. The figure spoke, and its words carried to every far flung edge of the crowd.

"Kernik has come, good people of Arkev City. Kernik is welcome among you. *I* am Kernik. Are you ready for the play?"

They had got their breath back. They started to shout: Yes, yes, they were ready.

The fiery figure half turned, looking west to the Duke's canopy before the golden Temple door. Kernik, Stealer of Scenes, executed a flamboyant, exaggerated, almost insulting bow. Then, straightening, he called out a name that Arkev might once have known, but knew no longer: Takerna, the Invocation.

It was to be the play Jy had put on at Svatza, the play Kernik Volk Volkhavaar had watched so avidly, and with such envy and greed, the play because of which, almost inadvertently, Jy had died.

Jy's effects had been excellent, approaching magic. But Kernik's effects were better, of course.

The magician spoke to the crowd, briefly, telling them a little of what they would see. Then he stepped back, and seemed to melt into space. As the people exclaimed, something new, something even more awesome and strange began to happen.

It was the moon.

Sinking she had been, slender as a bow, beyond the distant towers. Now she rose from those same towers, and returned incredibly the way she had gone.

Only the ignorant did not know the moon for what it was—a silver boat with the goddess riding in it, a boat with black sails and the wings of a gigantic swan. As the moon came overhead, she came groundwards too; her radiance swelled, filling the court and all the streets about it with a cold, white, flaming light. The torches dimmed and flickered out. The crowd gasped and here and there fell on its knees. The moon came out of the sky and hovered above the Sun Court, just as they had always imagined it, silver-sided, silken-sailed, swan-winged, and in it a goddess in robes of ice and metal with a smoke-blue cloud for her hair.

Music played, wonderful music, though no musicians were seen. The moon leaned on her pale, azure hand, dreaming, and below, the stage grew into the grassy plateau of a mountain, where a shepherd lay sleeping among his calamine flock.

Presently the moon spied him; a smile enhanced her lilac mouth. She stepped out of her moon-boat, and descended the air like a stairway of glass, white blossoms falling from her robes. The shepherd woke, and saw her, and threw himself down, afraid. But the moon was intent on other things than worship. She clasped the shepherd to her, all the length of her gleaming body, and the hillside and the moon-boat were consumed in the indigo conflagration of their union, leaving behind only torchless darkness.

Now came a rose-red glow: the dawn. The moon lady fled from it beneath an arch of rock. Shortly a mist evolved and hid her, and a chorus of creatures appeared, men with the heads of wolves, stags, ravens—not masks, for the eyes moved, the ears twisted, the skin wrinkled, the teeth were wet and bright. The chorus started to relate, irreverently, how even the Lady of the Moon was not immune from that universal fate of women—childbearing. However, the two stags began to remember a doe they had in common, and to do battle with their antlers, bellowing, and the wolves began to creep up on them, hungry tongues lolling, and the three ravens, professing boredom, unfolded wings and flew off into the sky, out of sight. Finally, a dreadful cry from the rock put wolves and stags to flight. The mist cleared, and there, alone, lay a baby beginning to sob and kick, a baby visibly shining, like a lamp.

Shepherds discovered it. There were various jokes, including a talking sheep, walking upright and being rather garrulous, which bore something of the resemblance to the Duke of Arkev, a thing the crowd, even glamorized as they were, did not overlook and raucously applauded, while the soldiers were noticed grinning. The Duke, missing the reference, naturally, laughed. His wife wore a malignant smile. Woana was too spellbound to giggle. She had not even noticed how her cat Mitz had left her lap and hidden under her chair.

Indeed, everyone was utterly ensorcelled. Including the unseen soul of Shaina on the lintel, though a kind of vague horror was laid on her, too.

The tale continued, and the mesmerizing illusions with it. When the sun rose, irregularly, on the pinnacle of the Temple, swelling into a great yellow orb, gilding the court impossibly with the true magnificence of day, the priests themselves turned pale. Out of the orb galloped the golden chariot drawn by its six saffron horses, in an auriole of clouds and rays. The sun was a fat man; huge and blazing he leaned down over the city, and when his rage came, several citizens scurried for cover. Lightning and thunder ripped across the sky. The sentence was pronounced—the Solar King, in his shame, would rise no longer. Then came a darkness without stars or moon, a darkness like a canopy, and the torches burned up again about the court, curiously relighting themselves, pink and pointed as swords.

About this time Shaina sensed Dasyel pass near her, below, crossing the court. He could not be seen, such was the illusion the magician had thrown over him like a cloak, but a moment later he apparently materialized, as all the rest of Kernik's troup had done, and became the hero of the story, as before in Svatza Town.

There was a special magic to Dasyel, as there was to Yevdora the Star-Maiden, and Roshi the Sun because they were living things, not merely illusions. Though the crowd knew none of this, some part of them sensed it. They responded to the hero and heroine, not merely for their looks, and to the Sun King, not merely for the ethereal melody he coaxed from a pipe when his terrifying wrath was spent.

Dasyel's voice, when he spoke so faultlessly, so immaculately, the words of the play, rang in the soul-breast of Shaina like the long unsounded notes of some eternal music, and even her dim apprehensions left her.

Dragons Dasyel fought, dragons more appalling than the dragon that had nonplussed Old Ash's village, beasts of such bone and bane and nightmare that women fainted when they saw them. Roads Dasyel travelled, roads of cloud and fire, that were drawn with unseen brushes on

the sky. There was no mending now in the brilliant armor
that he wore; his sword was truly a serpent, and the Star-
Maiden came to him in her dress of sparks, riding a carriage of white zircons drawn by a team of doves.

To watch him was pain to Shaina, sweet pain, like silver
wires piercing her. Little by little, the sorcery and the play
had washed away from her until she saw only him, one
bright figure moving in a mist. Everything she forgot, even
what she was and where she was, even Kernik, the Cruel
One.

When the end came, the great and daffodil heart of returning sun, the moistureless golden rain which fell, the
flowers which sprang up across the court, showering their
multicolored petals on the heads of the delighted audience,
Shaina lay dreaming, half asleep with love, drunk with it,
on the lintel of the Temple door.

The dark night had worn thin, like cloth, to a lucent
blueness. Soon an actual dawn would flood once more the
shining streets, and the Festival would be done. For now,
the pallid torches splashed and beat on their poles,
catching the wild glee of the stamping, vociferous crowd,
howling on the walls and scaffolding, tossing coins from
balconies, jewellery from windows, screaming in the
Square for the Duke to award the prize—not one, but
two, three, four bags of gold; no, a crown, a robe of gold,
or, maybe, the Duke's golden chair and all it symbolized.
Oh, yes, Kernik the Clever Showman was to be deified.
Never in all the world had such a play been known.

Duke Moyko was embarrassed.

Several times during the performance he had caught
himself with his mouth slithering open, his eyes popping.
And now this frightful demand that he make such unnec-
essarily extravagant gifts to a mere troup leader. Really, it
was too much; these ignorant fools with their noise. The
thing had been very good, very entertaining, but it was
just cunning and tricks, surely. . . .

Then there was a purple presence, very close, bowing
elaborately as before—such vulgarity and lack of finesse.
The Duke ran an imperial glance over the man, the incredibly rich robe with its embroideries, the tall saffron
hat. How pale, deadly pale, the face was, the smiling
mouth like a wound, a gash, the gold-rimmed eyes as pitiless, sunken and fixed as the eyes of some murderer just
plucked from the gallows—Moyko caught himself, and

said, a jot too fast: "Well, Kernik, as you hear, you've taken the prize."

"Not quite," said Kernik.

Baffled, the Duke somehow did not wish to press for further enlightenment.

"A very long work," he remarked patronizingly, "but skillful I will say." And he turned to summon the traditional bounty, and found it already at his elbow impatient to be given, the one fat bag, with, all around it, the brooches, pins, rings and other costly gew-gaws of Moyko's court. Curse it, now he must also give something, he supposed, and squeamishly cast about his person for an item that would look priceless and was not. However, the unequivocal crayoned mouth cut him short.

"Pray don't think to load me with gifts, my lord. I come from Volkyan Plain, and there honor is worth more than gold. I will take nothing, not even the prize. The approbation of Arkev City is reward enough for me, and for my children, the actors."

The crowd swallowed its voice a moment, then broke into an astonished paean. The Duke looked faintly startled, but not at this odd behavior, more at—

"Volkyan," said he. "*Volk*-yan?"

"I think," murmured Kernik the Prince of Conjurers, "your most worthy lordship has guessed my other name. I am called Volk by some. Volk Volkhavaar."

Somewhere inside Duke Moyko's belly a worm seemed to wake and writhe. His eyes burned, but he could not take them from the stranger's horrible lips.

Under Princess Woana's chair, the cat Mitz arched her back and laid flat her ears, but no one saw.

Even Shaina, lying like smoke on the golden lintel, saw only the face of Dasyel, charmingly smiling at the accolades of the crowd, offering homage to beautiful Yevdora, his blue-green, green-blue eyes cool-cold as certain pale gems on the tray of prizes.

Now the Duke was rising to his feet. He was making a speech, the people were yelling and throwing their hats heavenward. Music had been struck up again, and an impromptu yet exhilarated dance had broken out like a fever.

Where was the Duke going with Kernik the Clever Showman? Wherever it was, the Duke's people sanctioned it. Suddenly the Duke was riding in his golden chair on

the shoulders of the crowd, Moyko making flaccid nervous
motions; his narrow wife and blushing daughter next.
Then Kernik was lifted, nodding, smiling like a kind father, and presently the young actor, the lovely actress;
even the fat sun somehow hoisted and born along. Where
had the rest of Kernik's numerous bizarre troop vanished
to? No one noticed. Sorcery spiked the morning as the py-
rotechnic saltpeter had spiked it on previous days.

It was the palace they were making for. It seemed,
though the Festival of the Sun was over, it would be going
on in spite of itself. Even the priests were moving that
way, even the veiled girls from the Moon Temple; all
Arkev swarming south.

Shaina stirred like a breeze, and followed them.

Bewitched, she did not know it.

Somewhere in the middle of the human surge, colorless,
unwitnessed, unfelt and undreamed of, she settled in the
space beside Dasyel and kept pace with the men who carried him.

Girls were throwing flowers up to him, tearing off the
keepsakes of lovers and offering them—gold and silver
caught the new dawn fresh in the east.

Shaina drifted beside him. The thrown flowers fell
through her. She touched his hair and his shoulders
musingly. She perceived the dawn, but it meant no special
thing to her; no warning, no urging to return.

The crowd burst out into the Great Square before the
palace. A feast was being called for. The whole city
seemed in turbulent motion, the actual towers and roofs
swaying and clamoring.

The Duke, the Duchess and the Princess Woana were
borne to their very doors. Next moment they were inside,
the soldiers laughingly holding back the laughing press.
But Kernik was in the Duke's hall also, Kernik and his actors, and, all at once, the doors flew shut with a bang.

∗ 14 ∗

Kernik knew what he was doing, Kernik Volk Volk-havaar. He liked gestures and symbols, for his life rested on them. He liked to exercise his power in this fashion, a little at a time, casting out his shimmering net, tightening the strings, then drawing off again, the way a cat plays with a mouse. Run, mouse, see how far you can get when Volk lifts his paw. Not far.

Volkhavaar had already taken it all in, the fleshy-brained Duke, his acid wife, the plain, characterless daughter.

The induced dreams Moyko had been having had served their turn admirably. Squirming, trying to retain his dignity and stop his knees shaking, the Duke said:

"You are—er—*most* welcome. You must breakfast with us. Such an excellent performance—I highly recommend the ducks' eggs . . . a little wine?"

Volkhavaar had hung a very subtle illusion on himself, this time. He seemed extremely tall, upright, of a pristine and ominous darkness. Somehow the Duke, even the Duchess, received the impression that he, rather than they, had a right to sit in this massive hall, tended by bowing servants, dipping his claws in the silver fingerbowls, that perhaps (whisper it) the room and the food were not quite good enough for him. The Duchess found herself talking charmingly, listening to his every word as though drops of gold fell from his obnoxious slash of a mouth, attempting to—yes, actually—*ingratiate* herself into his good opinion. Every so often she would realize this with a shudder, and could only assuage her horrified surprise by thinking: But of course, he is such a *witty* man, such excellent breeding—obviously a prince disguised and travelling the roads at a whim. A fascinating eccentric. Even the manner in which he holds his knife is vastly superior to Moyko's manner of holding that utensil. And, no doubt, he recognizes *my* worth, just observe the way he looks at me. And,

123

extraordinarily flattered and flustered, the Duchess giggled in a startlingly unpleasant spasm of girlishness.

Woana huddled in her place, her eyes on the plate. Mitz had run off and could not be found. Woana guessed Mitz's desertion due to the presence of the fearsome stranger. She herself was terrified of him, she could not expressly say why. Just a glimpse of that thin, taloned hand poised above the table, sent clammy dashes of loathing and fright through every inch of her. And his name—hadn't her father said something about a marriage? Gods protect her, she who had given up so long ago all dreams of such, she would rather die than be bound in wedlock to Volk Volk-havaar. Sometimes, however, shyly, her scared eyes stole to the three other guests. The young man and the young woman both abashed her equally. She admired them for their beauty, but yearned for nothing from them. Life had trained her to bear her solitude. Now, seeing a handsome man, she looked at him as another would glance briefly at the blinding sun, as if at something alien and special, with which no contact might ever be expected. The fat actor, though, caught her attention and did not intimidate. Something about his solidity, the laughter lines about his mouth, his brown cheerful skin, comforted her. He had been a wondrous god up in the unbelievable chariot, all fire. And so cleverly he had played, and so cleverly produced amethyst eggs and blue birds out of the air. Surely such a fine, gentle, wholesome man could not be the friend of Kernik Volk—and if he were, maybe she was misjudging the actors' leader.

Outside, trestles had been set in the Great Square, barrels and dishes carried forth. Crowds were feasting and drinking, and toasting the Duke, and toasting Kernik the Clever Showman. How this had come about, Woana was uncertain. It was unlike her father to be generous to the people, but somehow the strange tall man had persuaded him ... and how uneasy the Duke was seeming about it.

Woana became suddenly aware of a muddy smouldering glare fixed, as it appeared, right on her—the eyes of Volk. Nervous water swelled in her own eyes, and her lips trembled, until she saw that in fact that malevolent gaze—and, indeed, malevolent it was—had been directed past her. In a shadowy corner of the room, among the drapery of heavy tapestries, Woana thought she glimpsed, only for a moment, another shadow, not dark but silver.

Woana blinked, and the shadow seemed to fade with her blinking.

Duke Moyko yawned. The idea of sleeping had come suddenly and demandingly into his mind. He had been up all night, had he not, and the noise of the crowd was tiresome, and the heat of the day bore down on him like a furry cloud. And there was that fat man playing on his pipe, playing like a nightingale in the broad light of day, a soft meandering tune, the sound of streams and woods, and how pleasant it would be to stretch out in that green shade, so good to lie flat on the pillowy, verdant bosom of Mother Earth and—

A clatter woke the Duke. He had dropped his goblet and his head had fallen dough-heavy on his breast. That wife of his had riveted him with an aqueous stare. Had he been snoring? Well, no matter, he was Duke Moyko and—

"Beloved Husband," said the Duchess, rising, "I think that I and your daughter will be going up to our rooms for a little rest. We cannot keep our eyes open," she added with measureless scorn.

"Just as you like," said the Duke, gazing swimmingly about. And there was Volk Volkhavaar smiling graciously at him. The pit of the Duke's belly turned cold, yet he thought to himself: He is a well-bred man. He understands the niceties. I had better be polite. Of course, it would take more than a few silly dreams to influence me, but rather safe, than sorry. Now what was I going to say?

"That is most kind," said Volkhavaar. "I am both honored and grateful for your invitation. I see that not idly do men praise, far and wide, the bounty of the Duke of the Korkeem."

What have I said? the Duke asked himself anxiously, but he could not recall. Obviously he had been offering hospitality to the overpowering—no, no, the regal—guest, the last thing he wanted or intended, although, perhaps— Duke Moyko ceased wrangling with himself. He wiped his hot face with a silk cloth, and lurched out of the hall and up the stairs, the usual tail of servants scurrying after. Aloft, on the great soft bed, he sank gratefully into hog-like slumber.

Kernik Volk kissed the Duchess's hand. His lips were cold and foreboding, but somehow it did not seem to matter. Why, he was quite handsome, in an unusual sort of way, though it would take, of course, a discerning, sensitive woman, a woman with a feeling for hidden talents and concealed worth, to spot the fact.

Woana attempted to creep out, like a little, grey, awkward mouse, unseen, around the wall. Volkhavaar naturally saw, however, let her get just so far, and then pounced. His hand fell lightly on her arm, and she seemed to feel teeth crunching together in her backbone.

"Hurrying away so fast, timid princess? And I hoped that we were going to be friends."

"I—I—I—" stammered Woana, "w-want to find my Mitz. She may be lost."

"Run along then," said the magician, and with a friendly, diabolical squeeze of her flesh, he let her go. "We shall have plenty of time to get better acquainted at a later hour. And besides, I have some business to attend to."

Woana fled. Her heart was in her mouth. She rushed into her lonely room and barred the door. But she was not comforted by this act, for somehow she guessed bolts and bars meant nothing to the terrible stranger. She tried to think of a suitable prayer, but no words came. And soon, despite herself, a great, deep somnolence gushed in at the window and covered her.

A curious slumber that was. Heavy and honey-sweet. It was falling like a warm, purple snow on Arkev. Not only the Duke and Duchess dormant, not only Woana, but throughout the whole palace, the Square, the Temples and the houses, the wharves and markets all about, excuses were being made to sprawl in the shade and sleep. Even on the river, the ships were drowsing. Even dogs had collapsed over bones, even birds lay like folded papers on the roofs. Arkev, busy, bright Arkev, supine in a lavender haze as if a cloud had settled on her, and from her chattering, bell-ringing, dog-barking, hammer-and-anvil streets, rose only now one sun-quenched and luxurious snore.

There were a few still unsleeping.

Just five.

And of these five, perhaps only two were truly awake.

About the tapestried walls the servants lolled. Roshi, the fat man, had set down his pipe and sat staring blindly; next to him, Yevdora sat, blind as he, her yellow hair plaited full of stars. Dasyel stood at the room's end in the shadow, still as a tree when all life has left the forest and no winds blow.

Volk Volkhavaar, perfectly motionless also, in the

Duke's gold chair, waited like a cat at a rat-hole. Then he saw it, as he had seen it previously, though at first he gave no sign. Dasyel, who had lost his shadow, suddenly again possessed one. A silver shadow, and not much like himself.

Volk's eyes narrowed a fraction. His mouth narrowed, smiling.

"Once upon a time," said Volk softly and aloud, "a young witch—I shall not name her, not knowing or needing her name—spied a young man, and she said to herself: I like the look of him; I will go after him. Yet, not being an ordinary maiden, but a witch, she did not travel the road on her firm, slim feet and with her long, long hair tied up in a kerchief and her belongings on her back, oh no. She made a soul-spell, and it was her spirit she sent on her errand. And round and round him her spirit beat like the moth round the lamp." Behind Dasyel, the silver shape was transfixed and faintly flickering. Volk's grimace of a smile widened. "It seems that, despite all her cleverness, the young lady did not know how bright her unspotted maiden's soul would shine, and how fragrant would be the scent of it. It seems no one told her: Beware, someone has an eye for such brightness, and nose for such scent. It seems too that no one warned her she should be back inside herself by dawn or people might notice. Or maybe the intelligent but ill-informed young lady dwells alone? Does she, then, understand that only a short span may she be absent, or the magic cord, which joins soul to flesh—" Volkhavaar rose, and went forward across the room, appropriately snapping his awful fingers to emphasize the word—"*Snaps!*"

The dazzle in the air swirled abruptly into motion. Up and around and out of the nearest window it went.

Volk, grinning like a wolf, leapt to the sill. He raised his arms. They were wings. Lifted his head. It was a bird's cruel, hooked mask. Volkhavaar was a falcon, and the falcon flew up into the air with a derisive scream, staring out the sun, stooping after the perfumed scent of his aerial prey, which was Shaina's soul. Just as a man, important matters set aside for a while, goes out to find pleasant recreation.

* 15 *

The dawn, which came with such wizardry and wildness to Arkev, broke on Old Ash's village in the valley in its usual way. To begin with.

Women went to the well and the cookpots, men to the cattle. Fires were kindled and the proper words spoken over them. Then came the first discord. Who could mistake the tones of Old Ash's wife screeching and railing at her slave?

Young Ash, still sober, had gone to see the goats; Old Ash had strode out into the morning to cut wood by the stream. Downstairs came the wife, looking for the slave to be busy—bringing water, laying the fire, getting the porridge ready—and there, by the Mother, the slothful horror still lay, flat on her back, beside the clinkers of the unlit hearth.

"Wake up, you heaven-accursed good-for-nothing! Wake up!" cried Old Ash's wife, but the slave did not stir. Old Ash's wife kneeled down and gave Shaina a rough and brutal shaking and yelled in both her ears and presently flung over her the contents of the water pitcher. After this the wife's voice rose to an extraordinary pitch, which caused even those who knew her to marvel. As it was remarked later, not a man or beast could slumber through such an alarm, and even those asleep in the graveyard on the hill were said to have wakened and turned over. Only the slave girl continued to lie senseless on her bed of rags, her hands limp and her eyes fast shut, and never even a groan out of her.

The priest from Kost was eating new-baked bread in Mikli's house, when the commotion developed to its ultimate crescendo.

"And who can that be?" he asked.

"Old Ash's wife," said Mikli, "requesting something of Old Ash's slave."

But a few moments later, the altercation took on a new note—grief.

128

People went out into the street, and there Old Ash's wife stood, beating her breast and staring up resentfully at the sky full of gods.

"Oh!" she shrieked, "The slave is sick! All the good food wasted I have given her, and the good money Old Ash paid for her. Oh, a thousand tears!"

The priest too had come out into the street by this time. The little crowd stood aside respectfully to let him pass. He walked up to Old Ash's wife and looked at her until she stopped her noise.

"Where is your husband?" asked the priest.

"Cutting wood by the stream, heaven defend him."

"And what is your trouble with the slave?"

"She is sick, Father," said the woman, "Wicked, graceless monster that she is."

"Sick of what?" asked the priest.

"I don't know to be sure. The best of everything she's always had. It's not a fever, but she lies there asleep, and she never moves when I shake her."

The crowd murmured at this. The priest said:

"Someone go for Old Ash," and went by the wife and into the house and up to the hearth where Shaina lay.

The doorway was quickly full of faces, blocking out the sunlight.

The priest knelt next to Shaina. He looked at her intently with his observant eyes; he touched her throat a moment and her wrist, and then leaned and held the golden sun around his neck to her mouth. After a second he took the gold thing away and looked at it. He pulled at his lip.

'You,' he was saying to his belly, 'you, with your dinners and breakfasts and suppers, you and your: Question the slave tomorrow, or the day after. . . . Now see what's happened.'

Just then Old Ash came in like a black bear, touched his brow to the priest, and stared in perplexed distress at his expensive property lying so inert by the hearth.

"What's wrong with her, Father?"

"I am thinking," said the priest, "that she is no longer breathing." A gasp from the doorway. "Also I am thinking," said the priest, "that she is not dead. Perhaps you have had a witch among you, and never known. How long have you owned the girl?"

"Something like a year, maybe," said Old Ash.

"There is a witch-woman on Cold Crag, too, is there not?" demanded the priest, who missed little.

Whispers in the doorway now, Old Ash lowering his eyes.

"Indeed not, Father. A witch? No, no."

"Very well," said the priest. "I can see the bottom of the pool quite clearly, despite all the stones you are throwing in."

On the wrist of the slave girl was a strip of linen no one had ever noticed, except for the priest. Quickly his tubular fingers worked it loose, and his intent gaze went up the wrist and down.

Yes, as he had guessed. Two tiny, almost-healed scars, the marks of two sharp, little teeth like those of a fox or a cat. A witch's familiar.

"And what does the Lady of Cold Crag ask for her favors, her love charms and sleep potions? Different prices? Or is it always the same. Who here has paid with blood?"

A startled, stifled shout. Then a woman called from the back of the crowd, boldly: "*That* price no one has ever paid in this village."

"I hope you are truthful," said the priest, rising up, stern and awesome in his red, "Though I don't believe anyone else has made sorcerous bargains. Only this girl here, and she must be dealt with this very midnight."

"Dealt with?" burst out Old Ash in alarm. "My slave is very valuable—how can I afford another if I must be rid of her?"

"You will do as I tell you," said the priest with a dreadful look, "unless you wish to begin a plague of vampires in this valley."

The sky was a hollow bell, ringing with blueness, Burning vapor trails of broken cloud below, like blossom on a lake, upper air thin as eggshell, pierced with fragile rays like the slender strings of a harp. Through its alleyways of soundless sapphire fled Shaina's soul.

There had been flight before, but not like this flight. This flight was an abandonment to terror, a silent scream of anguish and despair. Before, she had known, had flown in time and out of time, so fast she could not reckon, hauled home by the chain which bound her, safe into her flesh, hidden from the peril of night.

Now, night pursued her, or a piece of it, a jet-black fal-

con like a torn black sail on the sky-sea wind. No chance
now, none. Too late. He could unravel time as her spirit
could, she could not shake him off. And the morning wide
over the land and her body in the village doubtless discovered, uninhabited, defenceless. Shaina, Shaina, what have
you done?

She had known there was magic in the air of Arkev, but
she had not heeded it. She had lain in the stupor of her
love, and the magic had bound her like corded rope. She
had followed Dasyel, thinking of nothing, recollecting
nothing, seeing only him. She had ceased to exist, or so it
seemed to her. She had become, in total abnegation, a part
of the aura of Dasyel, a sigh breathed from his lungs. Not
until the magician looked straight at her, knifed her with
his eyes and his soft and abominable words, telling her,
telling her he knew her, saw her, had her in the trap, not
until that moment, did the soul of Shaina wake. Then,
magic, joy, love, all forgotten, Shaina fled, but with no
hope. The torn, black sail ran leisurely and certainly behind her. The dark one was playing at a chase, eeking it
out. When he grew tired, he would have her easy as a
smile, Volk Volkhavaar, the Cruel.

And the chain which linked her to herself, that beckon-
ing pull was weaker. She had been gone too long, and
there was little strength left in it to urge her nearer, reel
her in as before, swifter than thought. Yet still, hopelessly,
she fled on.

She passed through a cloud like smoking fleece, and on
the other side of it the sky was full of birds.

At first, even in wild panic, she put them from her mind
as natural innocent things. Silver swift, she darted over
them and under them, their wings ebony flashes through
her ghostly skin.

But the birds did not leave her. They clustered and
flocked nearer. Falcons. Their wings beat now in a black
whirlwind across her eyes, her head. Their faces were all
exactly similar, savage, open-beaked triangles of fury.
Their claws raked at her and, though they could not tear
her astral tissues, they smothered and confused her, and,
with her insubstantial arms, she tried to beat them away.
Her eyes no longer contained sky nor destination, only the
darting of pinions and talons and raucous, pointed tongues
like bloody daggers. In vain she struggled to win free,
twisting, turning, rising and sinking. She understood at last

who had sent the birds, or conjured them, or filled the air
with their illusion.

How long she fought, fought to see her way, to evade
the horror, she did not know. At length, caught in a spinning storm-tunnel of black feathers, she plummeted earthwards.

The branches of trees tore vainly at her. She was dashed
through iron trunks, shadows, into the viridian depths of a
forest. She sank like a mist on the ground, and the hurri-
cane of falcons was gone.

Cool the forest was, and somber, filled by the rilling of
streams, the dripping notes of small birds. Yet the menace
was there too, still intimate with her, still in her ears like a
high-pitched, distant cry, forever prolonged.

Shaina's soul rose from the grass, darting from tree to
tree, a white whisper in the shade. A stream lay before her
and she spangled over it. Pebbles spangled in reply from
its bottom; pleasant the forest was, but the hunter was
close behind, she knew, she knew.

Then the bird song fell quiet about her, the leaves
ceased rustling, as if their motion had been cut in two.

Shaina looked back, over her ghost shoulder.

Nothing. Oh, but she knew.

Faster she moved, fast as the flicker of a lizard's tongue.
The trees ran by as if also in flight, green flight, but backwards to greet what pursued her. And now a new sound
replaced the old sounds which had died.

Insidious thunder. Under her feet, in the boles of the
trees. Yes, the hooves of black horses pounding hard as
rock on the ground.

Up Shaina flew, into the topmost boughs, beyond them,
seeking again, involuntarily, the sky.

The sky was open, yet, at the curving edges of its bowl,
black falcons, myriads of them, like small black clouds, or
black, shining stars, made to darken day as the white stars
were made to lighten the night. They did not come near
her now, only circled and clung to the edges of the sky
bowl, calling to each other, or to her, shepherding her; the
clever hounds of the magician.

Once more poised in blue space, Shaina looked back.

And as she looked, out of the canopy of the forest, in a
shimmering explosion of leaves and broken boughs, like
some huge, malignant fish bursting upwards from an ocean,
the great chariots of the magician plunged into the air.

Black it burned, brilliantly and blazingly black. Six black horses pulled it, leaping, heaven-borne on the curved-back wings of eagles. Diamonds seared in their nostrils and sprays of flaming blood or ichor gushed from their jaws. Behind them, the fiery reins tied about his middle, two bronze whips with serpent tails in his black-clawed hands, stood a purple man, with the head of a wolf.

This sight was terrible, more terrible than words convey, for words are cowards as men are, and hide things as men do.

The head of the wolf grinned; the teeth were yellow and each one pointed.

The living whips cracked in the man's hands and the horses flared forward and the wheels of the chariot spat off lights, and Shaina fled on.

Why did she fly? Could she believe that this being was to be avoided? No. She fled because she was reduced to that ultimate shrivelled mindless terror that flies only because it no longer has the power to think, to reason, for reason would say: You are lost, be still.

Volkhavaar, the sadistic, the pitiless. He had not mislaid all his pleasure in human fear. Across the meadows of the sky he chased the maiden's soul, while behind him Arkev, insolent Arkev soon to be his and his god's, lay sleeping and dreaming the dreams he had left there. And gradually the sun turned westwards and the sky deepened to the shades of love.

"See, moth, it doesn't pay to flutter round the lamp. Not *my* lamp, maiden-moth. Not *mine*."

The woman came first, up the hill from the village.

They were placed alternately, a wife, then a young girl—a virgin.

The married women each carried a torch, the girls each carried a sprig of white flowers plucked in the fields. They were silent, these red-lit white ones, and behind them walked the priest.

The priest swung a censor, a censer of silver from Kost. Aromatic steams issued from it. The priest spoke prayers as he went, his face set as hardened wax. Also, he carried a sword.

Last came the men, tapers in their fists, and three goats led by a rope and drawing, on some planks of wood

lashed together, something motionless and slight, the black
hair of which trailed over the ground behind it.

Everyone was well versed in what must be done. The
priest had been teaching them all day, while the slave girl's
body lay quiescent as a doll in the street, inside a ring of
burning torches stuck firmly in the earth, and with a silver
piece wedged between her teeth to stay her, if suddenly
the roaming demon she had become, should return.

Old Ash, grey and drawn, sat on a stone in the street,
gripping his knees, cursing his luck. A deadly, close silence
held the village, and at sunset the mountains had seemed
washed with blood.

Now the sky was long quenched by midnight, and the
young moon riding it, and not a breath of wind on the
hills.

It was to the graveyard they were going, and past it a
little way, for the slave girl's body, contaminated as it was
by evil things, could not lie in holy ground.

Between the mounds they went, and upwards to a barren piece of land in the lea of rocks, where seldom anyone
came. Here they walked three times in a circle left hand,
three times in a circle right hand. The women spoke the
words the priest had told them. The torches burned in
their eyes.

Two men came forward and began to dig the harsh soil.
Soon a black gape stared up at them, and into this, thick
as snow, the maidens cast their flowers.

The chariot of Volkhavaar—illusion, reality, conjura-
tion—turned about beneath the moon, urging its silver
quarry west again, south again, as it had urged it all
through the deepening violet of evening, the cold hours of
night, playing the old game of cats with mice.

Did the soul still think at all? Did it remember anything
of itself? Yes, something. Even so late, the frenzied, in-
stinctive attempt to rejoin its flesh.

This Volkhavaar knew. Eventually he would bring down
his paw on the back of the soul, allow it to eddy away,
seep through roof or wall, back into body. Then, he would
destroy body and soul together; his latest sacrifice in the
name of his genius, the neglected god of Arkev, Takerna—Sovan Tovannazit.

So gradually, he was letting her get a little nearer home.
Mile by hard-won mile. Souls cannot feel weariness, yet he

never doubted the girl's soul felt it. He grinned with his unspeakable jaws.

Then he saw the light, red as rubies, on the hill.

He was quick, Volk had always been so. And he had learned, since the advent of his power, the rites for many an occult office, whether to be rid of darkness, or to call it. He saw at once what they were at, below him. And he knew at once for whom they troubled.

Werewolf, he slavored, with a laughter bottomless as death, and reined in his grizzly team. Let her go, the little moth. Let her go and watch. Someone was doing his work for him.

Maybe he hated Shaina, whose name he did not know or need. She loved Dasyel and had sought him out, one of the magician's toys, his possession. She had dared covet a thing of Volkhavaar's. Now he stood in the sky, invisible, clothed in his black hate, and when he had seen enough, sneering, he turned away, back to the greater work he must accomplish in the city.

It was like a net lifted from her, a fetter of lead broken suddenly.

All at once she was free of him, free of his terror and his might. Free to think and to feel. A vast shadow, hungry and inimical as night itself, had fallen away and left her, maddened, exhausted—yet *unharmed*.

A moment's wild thankfulness, followed by a moment of frantic disbelief. Why? Why had he spared her?

Then a new dread seized her, not like the first, a dread hollow as a grave, and with a grave's raw, vile smell to it. Every other thing, past or anticipated, was blotted out.

She experienced the tug, the pang, the actual pain of the magic cord writhing through her as if wordlessly screaming to her. And she was descending, haphazardly and in confusion as on that previous return, rushing towards Old Ash's house, though on the hill, a light seemed to shout to her: Here, Shaina, here!

She heard something then indeed, a groaning, wailing lament. It rose from the village, from the houses there, especially from the house of her master. She stared down, through rafter, roof and flagstone, into the space beneath the threshold, and there something formless and pale, lay moaning and weeping: the demon, warning of disaster and death, though only she, it seemed, could hear it.

Not a light in the village, and all the houses empty. She recognized this abruptly. Even she, her girl's body, was gone. And the mind-scream came again, the agonized tug towards the hill.

And she was going there, whatever she wished, being whirled into the torch-glare and the incense smoke that was like Arkev Fair, and yet was not.

'Shaina, I am here, here. See. This you have betrayed me to. I am your meaning and your life, as you are mine. But you left me, and look what they have done. Oh, look, look. Look down and see. This is your fault.'

Shaina froze on the air. She could not turn aside. Like a mother who sees her child spitted on a spear in front of her, while the soldiers hold her captive, Shaina, locked in the arms of night, must witness and comprehend all.

Souls cannot call aloud, souls cannot tear their skin with their nails, or wrench at the arms of men with their transparent hands. Souls cannot die and drowning know the sable pit as it gulps them. Souls cannot weep. Tell Shaina now these things: she will say otherwise.

The doll body of the slave lay before the priest on the cloak of its own black hair. The priest had raised a sword, a bright sword of bronze from Kost, its metal sacred and blessed. He kissed the blade and swung it high. It sliced the cloth of the dark, the fabric of the stars. It made the shape of a white wheel, turning russet as it came downwards and the brands stained it.

At the end of the lovely glittering stroke, it severed the mortal head of Shaina from her mortal shoulders.

The women of the village shrieked like birds caught in frightful snares.

The slave girl's blood ran crimson among the strands of her hair. The priest bent, and pushed the silver coin clenched between her teeth through into her mouth, then signalled. The men tip-tilted the wooden boards so that they slid over the lip and down into the flower strewn grave. They landed awkwardly, and the maiden's head rolled the length of her, coming to rest between her feet, and all her body was reddened by its passage.

"Fill in the mound," said the priest. He wiped his forehead, and his clever eyes were tired and sad. "Your village is safe now, and she is at peace."

Peace—oh, Shaina—*peace*—

✳ 16 ✳

The pre-dawn wind was striding up and down Cold Crag mountain, rattling the pines.

Somewhere on the slope, at the edge of a clearing, a grey stone house like a squat mossy boulder, with a smoke snake coiling on its twisted chimney. Inside, maybe, someone rocking, rocking in a birchwood chair among the skinny people-pillars, and a fox-red fire with a fire-red fox on the east side of it.

Now the wind was furling and curling about the round door, beating there like wings, asking to be let in.

The fox pricked its ears, and barked.

Someone looked at the fox, a grey boulder lady:

"Only the wind, worry-ears."

But again the fox barked, and now someone was listening too.

"Barbayat!" cried out the wind, in a thin, aching, anguished voice, "Barbayat, Barbayat, let me come in."

Barbayat, the grey lady, rose and went to her round door.

"Who is there?" she asked, eyes like flints, sharp enough to scratch you.

"You knew me once, Barbayat. Once you sought me out. Once you were my mother, Barbayat, you drank my life away. Your walls are too strong, I cannot come through. Let me in, or the wind will blow me out of this world."

"One moment," said the witch. She took a lump of white clay and drew on the floor with it a white shape, ancient and valid as earth. Then she opened her door.

In swirled a vapor, colored like moonlight, and the clay shape caught it in and held it fast, and the witch shut the door.

"Now you are safe for a while," said she, "while the magic on the floor contains you. It will lend you a voice

137

too, better than borrowing the voice of the wind. So tell me who you are."

The swirling in the clay ceased. A slender column straightened up. There stood Shaina, like a ghost, and the witch knew her.

"Something is missing," said Barbayat.

"The chain that bound me is broken," said Shaina's soul in a voice like the dry rustling of leaves. "Shall I tell you why, witch-lady? I went to the city, and the magician's magic trapped me as it traps all that place of Arkev. I saw only one face; I forgot my life and what I was. Then the magician found me. He hunted me across the sky and the land, I will not mention the terror of it, and then he let me go. In the village they could not wake my body, and there was a priest. He examined my wrist and discovered the marks your teeth left, Barbayat, Grey Lady, in my vein. They laid me on a sled of planks, they bore me up the hill. In the red light of the torches the priest swung the bright sword and smote my head from my body. Into the ground they threw me in two pieces, in among the flowers, and buried me with earth. When they were gone, I kneeled above the mound, I mourned at my own grave. I am dead. Dead, Barbayat, dead. Dead."

"Shaina," said the witch, "all ways I warned you. To beware of Volkhavaar, to return in time, to let no one see the wound I gave you."

"Is it the dust of a dry well you offer me then, when I ask for water? Is it the mouldy crumbs of last month's bread you put before me when I entreat you for food?"

"Soul," said Barbayat, "you are very strong. You cling to life when another would long since have been swept away to a different place. What do you suppose the Grey Lady can do for you?"

"You called me daughter," Shaina said, "I called you mother. Save me, my mother. Keep me in the world."

"Is it life, or still love you hunger for?"

"Both, both. In Arkev I saw him, called him. His spirit did not answer mine, as you told me it would."

"Maybe I deceived you a little," said the witch. "I will undeceive you now. Even by the enchantments of a magician, a body cannot live unless its soul exists too. Somewhere. But Dasyel casts no shadow, and this seemed ill to me, for he that goes shadowless, generally, something has taken his soul—in trade, or for other reasons. Firstly, I was not certain—so the Old Lady of Cold Crag seeks to excuse her encouragement of your dream. But I looked in the crystal, and presently I learned. The soul of Dasyel, and of others also, is imprisoned forever in the belly of Volkhavaar's black god, whose name, you note, even I do not utter. Soulless golems those captives will be until the day the magician tires of his toys; then their flesh he will destroy, and nothing of them will remain at all. You, poor maiden, have at least left to you your most precious part. Changed you will be, but not ended. The soul of Dasyel is eternally bewitched: in chains, blind, dumb, deafened; without consciousness or sentience, incapable of animation or affection. Even you, brave and stubborn as you are, cannot save him from that. I thought, when I understood your young man's fate, you would try only once, and so be safe. I thought you would go to him and—receiving no answer—despair and grieve, and get over your despair and your grief, for you were proud. Then you might seek me for the solace of spells, for there was a sorceress in you, so much I saw, waiting to be taught. What if you had? Freedom, if you had, and power, and maybe joy and lovers, too. But yours is the heart whose star rises only once, only one love, and that enduring, so much is evident. So let the winds of the Other World take you. It will be better in a while. The place that waits for you is sweet; no pain there, no struggle, no heartbreak. To linger is fruitless. You can never be one with him. The soul of Dasyel is *dead*."

Shaina's immaterial arms stretched out from her body, palms open, every finger rigid.

"No," said the passionless crackling un-voice which was all the witch's magic could lend her. "I want pain, I embrace it, and struggle and heartache. See, I open my arms to them. I won't lie down before Death and bare my throat for him. I too have teeth, I too have nails. I won't go off this earth and leave Dasyel in it trapped in a devil's guts. There is a way to all things. I will make a way. If I had lived, he might have preferred another, he might have frowned at me and turned aside. What does this matter? It is I who loved, not he. I will not leave him in a devil's guts. Now, tell me. Barbayat is clever. Surely there is some means she knows to keep me in this curse of a world. I will not go to any other land."

"That is how you are," said Barbayat. "I recall I told

you as much, once. Because the gate is barred, you must have it down."

And the witch smiled, and something fell away from her like a grey garment, and there were emeralds in her glances.

"There is a spell. Not any easy spell and not any easy existence to follow, but it will keep you here. Though perhaps your wish to remain is not strong enough after all, for this needs a will like diamond, hard and bright."

"Say it," said Shaina. "Let us see."

The witch spoke and Shaina listened and the fire huddled on the hearth.

"There now," said Barbayat. "There is a wolf and there are his jaws. Put in your hand."

PART FOUR

*The City
and Its Gods*

* 17 *

Dark was the city in the hour before dawn, pitch dark as the inside of a mole-hole. No lights burning: not a torch, not a lamp, not a beacon even, bright on the tower of a temple. The moon had set, the stars had hidden their faces behind fans of cloud. It was a long sleep that had held Arkev from the sunrise of one day to the sunrise of the next.

Some things had not slept.

Rats were busy on the wharves about their ratty business, glad of the oddly inactive watchmen. Owls had gone late hunting, and the slender cats of the merchants' quarter and the taverns had been here and there in the echoing streets, slipping like silken threads from shadow to shadow, serpent-headed under their point ears, and with a green flash in their glares for the moon, when she found them.

Up on a high gable, mostly still as black marble, one more cat was sitting, staring out over the forest of towers and roofs towards the east, as if looking for the dawn with her gem-stone eyes. This cat, at least, was not often abroad. This cat was a princess, being the companion of a princess of mankind. Generally, it was on swansdown pillows she slept. Why not at home in the palace, Mitz?

To the south, the pinnacles of the Duke's house dully shone; but some of the windows there, seemed erratically shining too, pale, pale shines of the most somber and insubstantial purple. When these gleams occured, Mitz laid flat her ears and spat, and her tail doubled itself and lashed like a snake on the gable. Oh, no, Mitz was not going home, even to her goddess Woana. Clever Woana who could do such wonderful things, such as producing food without first catching it: who could make light simply by causing a yellow flower to appear on white sticks of wax, and afterwards make darkness, simply by breathing on this same flower. Now and then, Mitz had noticed other people doing this, but no one, of course, did it *quite* as Woana did. Woana was the most talented, amazing and prodigious human in the world, and the most beautiful too. For Woana, if she had summoned them, those bright eyes in the sky would have danced down to earth; but naturally Woana was far too sophisticated to stoop to such a thing. Woana was, in fact, unrivalled, peerless. The reason being that Mitz belonged to her, and Mitz's feline ego would never consider that anyone, but the most sublime, could have acquired her own exceptional self.

Now, however, something was very wrong.

A presence had intruded on the smooth track of life, a shadow had been cast—dark, clammy, alien—and Woana, incredible though her attributes might be, had done nothing to get rid of it. With the true and unshakeable instincts of her kind, Mitz felt, Mitz knew, the tall, thin, purple man was to be feared, the way she feared and sidestepped ghosts and goblins and devils, but worse, far worse.

So, this is why she sat on the high gable, marble-still one minute, sizzling and grimacing the next, and wouldn't go home to her nice, soft bed.

And then something even stranger, even more insupportable, happened. Something which Mitz, with all her stores of catty wisdom, had never been warned of, never been prepared to expect.

Up went Mitz, head over heels.

Down came Mitz, shook herself convulsively, bared her teeth, and suddenly, claws asunder, head, legs and tail each thrust wildly at all the points of the compass, Mitz let out a catawaul to end catawauls. Even the owls paused and looked down, and the rats paused among the sacks of flour, and someone, someone dark and cruel, paused and listened behind purple-flickering palace windows.

Barbayat had cheated Shaina, yet Barbayat had taken her blood, and Barbayat, in some curious way, had loved her. No doubt it was true that for the slave she had seen the fiery crown of sorcery if not the chaplet of love. For Barbayat this day, near dawn, softly, told her the way, the dangerous, unlikely, almost obscene way she might remain in the world—no longer Shaina the maiden, black hair down her back, head high, waist slight and strong as willow, not this—but still aware, living, cased in flesh. Of a sort.

Dual, the spell was, two things.

First, since her motive for life remained the young man Dasyel, she must fly back to his vicinity, however ill-omened the place, however near the magician it would bring her. Continually, her hold on existence would weaken; then she must look at her love, refresh her will and her power in sight of him—if she could. If ever her loving flagged, her grasp on corporeality would also flag. Truly, her love was to be her life from this dawn onwards. And she wished to free him, but did not know how, knew only that, whatever else, if her task were ever accomplished, she must at last let go her borrowed hold on living, and fade out into that nebulous otherworld the witch had spoken of. Never now could she hope or dream of being the lover of Dasyel, the wife of him, the mother of his children, he the father of hers, left hand of right hand, right hand of left, corona of moon and sun of sky and heart's home. Never now, while day followed after day and the winds blew. Yet, the words still rang in her: I will not leave him in a devil's guts. Pared to spirit, her purpose remained like iron in the silver.

The second essential of the spell was deeper, more cloudy. She feared it, yet fear did not stop her. Pity too, she felt, and revulsion, and cold chills at maybe losing her identity forever.

Then the occasion presented itself. Close; convenient almost. Not the rats she had shunned, the owls, the sleeping pigeons, but, silken and sable, jade-eyed and beautiful and surely tame, surely—surely the one she had seen on the very lap of the Princess—a creature with access to the palace of Arkev.

The air seemed full of the spell, alive with it, painful with it. Her reluctance guttered out in confusion.

Shaina fell. She fell as a star falls or a bird with broken wings, burning, helpless and blind. Then there was an end to falling.

It was as if she were—what?—a scarf perhaps or a string of beads, folded small, coiled and compressed, and forced down into a tiny box too narrow for her, and the lid—horror, terror—was slammed shut.

She struggled. She struggled to breathe and to see and to *be*, to *continue*. Her arms, her hands—or, her eyes, where were her eyes? And her voice! A scream burst from her. But not precisely a scream.

And then all at once, the fight was over.

She lay curled, barely sane, in the unknown region, and tried to weep.

Then came something and brushed against her. Not physical, and not experienced physically. A consciousness.

Shaina flinched away, tried to hide, could not; sensed the other also trying to hide. Steadied herself, opened out. Waited; prompted.

Now, again. A thought. Not hers: a cat thought.

Shudderingly, both. Both somehow with a common tongue, since it was common ground they occupied, yet imagery very different and emotion almost without parallel.

No real agony, a sort of ache, a despair.

Shaina trying in some fashion to explain, to apologize. Aware the cat would like to claw her out, yet, with the innate, thorny poilteness of a cat, holding off. Then, an unlooked-for astonishing little exchange, as if Shaina could abruptly associate with the cat, the cat with Shaina. Empathy, understanding. The whole of it emerging with a kind of peculiar translation into cat-tongue, woman-tongue, for each simultaneously.

"Pardon me, I was desperate, as for a fishhead. Death was after me, the closer of eyes, cold-fur-bringer. Can you forgive me, share plate with me, mate with me? Meow—behold, I am a mouse before your claw."

"Never forgive. But maybe. Yes. Stroke me, I am upset. Kindly do not blink my eyes so fast and mind where you are putting my tail. What is this you are remembering? A man? How nicely his fur curls."

"May I stretch a little? I am cramped."

"Stretch if you must. Stretching is good, also washing. Ugh! Do not think, if you please, of jumping in a cold stream. Lick my paw. So much better. Ah! You have stretched too far. There go the memories of my last piece of liver, crowded out."

"I beg your pardon. I will not stay long."

"Where are we going? Be careful! Almost we fell from the gable. Let me do it: Tense, spring, leap. There. (*How* long is your long?) Wait. I don't wish to go that way."

"The palace? I must."

Cat's brain spitting, primitive allusions to shadows, darkness, the *man* . . .

"Volk will not harm you. He is an admirer of your kind. He will give you liver, and cream."

"You too, if you are still here."

Shaina finding a dream of dead mice hanging red on claws: Food. Shaina sick, turning the cat sick, the cat spinning round and biting her own tail on the parapet, meowing her discomfort and misery. Shaina somewhere distressfully saying she was sorry. Both brains blanking out. Into one, a white lover, into one, a dark lover. Dasyel and a snowy tom co-mingled. Common ground again. Silence, searching. Caution.

And all about, benighted Arkev, opening by soft degrees to summer sunrise.

* 18 *

The city woke.

The city recollected.

Or seemed to.

A husband had finally been found for the Duke's daughter, a powerful and magnificent prince from Volkyan Plain—by name, Volkhavaar. There would be celebrations and rejoicings. Gold coins would shower like spring rain, the fountains would run wine, both white and red.

The magician's sorcery had spun a spiderweb of memory in the night, in the long sleep.

Beneath his velvet canopy the Duke woke, feeling satisfied, portentous, somehow uneasy. . . . A good match, he had been clever to arrange it so well. But the man, charming, intelligent and remarkable though he was—no, no, Duke Moyko would not admit to being intimidated by him. The Duchess, meanwhile, was up early, bathing in rosewater, fixing pearls in her ears, powdering pinkly her sickly countenance, looking forward to greeting her son-in-law-to-be.

Woana, too, had recalled.

She lay huddled in her bed, twitching yet almost petrified, like a field mouse among the corn anticipating the scythe.

The door burst open. In swept her mother, all gauzes, like a liverish butterfly.

"What? Not up yet? Goodness me, Woana, where is your sense of occasion? We mustn't keep our intended waiting, must we?" she added archly.

Closet doors flung wide.

"*This* one, I think," cried the Duchess, dragging forth an exaggerated creation of bitter lime silk edged with vermilion. Presently, doused with water and scents, laced into her hideous finery, her lank hair crimped and tonged and bound with a tall fillet of opals, her arms fettered with

bracelets and ten rings on her hands, down the stairway
Woana was propelled. Into the hall.

How dark the hall was. Even the morning windows
burned with a darker light, their panes of colored glass ob-
scuring rather than interpreting the sun.

And there, by a window—

Black and purple and gold he was, like a fabulous insect
with a poisonous sting. He took her hand, his own like ice.
Black claws, mouth sketched in old blood, eyes like pits.

At the table. Damask and fine linen, silver eating tools
and jewelled cups, all dulled by that indefinable, dark
sheen. Shadows everywhere, seeming clotted close about
them all. The lord from the Volkyan ate elegantly, spar-
ingly, but with enjoyment. He cracked the brittle bone of a
chicken's leg between his teeth. Behind him stood his three
servants, the young girl and the young man and the fat
man. How perfectly still they were, how blank their faces,
almost as if . . .

Oh, if only Mitz were here, her small, pretty Mitz. That
would be some comfort. Woana dropped a knife clumsily
from her trembling fingers, and Lord Volkhavaar looked
at her, and she noticed how he delicately sucked the marrow from the bone.

"Whom did you say, my dear son-to-be?" asked the
Duchess, earlobes tinkling.

"Why, most youthful mother, a deity of my own house,
my patron god, to whom I exclusively offer my devotions."

"And a shrine, here in Arkev?"

"Indeed yes, most youthful mother-sister. But a shrine
in sad need of repair."

The Duke cleared his throat. He did not want to be ex-
cluded.

"Some more wine for my kin Volkhavaar," he instruct-
ed, but it was the young man at Volkhavaar's elbow—his
son?—nephew?—servant?—who moved to fill the gold
goblet. Curiously, the Duke's own servants had vanished.
"I didn't catch the name," the Duke said.

"Ah, my patron has many appellations," smiled Volkhavaar. "The chiselling on the lintel of the shrine is this:
Sovan Tovannazit. Or maybe you have heard his other
name, Takerna?"

When this word was spoken, a black lightning appeared
to go over the table. The tapestries eddied out from the
walls, the wings of birds seemed to beat at the windows.

The Duchess's smile was fixed, the Duke stared about him. Woana clenched her hands beneath the table to a bloodless white. Volkhavaar bowed.

"In the great Sun Temple of Arkev, the famous Temple where the sun himself rests a moment on the pinnacle at noon, perhaps a corner may be found—some obscure, dark corner—where my god might stand for those of us who wish to honor him? Or do I presume too much on my father and my mother?"

"I will summon the priests," said the Duke. "I will explain the matter, and council them."

The Duchess cried:

"Praise the gods, Woana, that your excellent betrothed is also pious."

And soon, the priests came. The red and golden priests of the Sun Temple, the blue and silver priests of the Temple of Stars, the white veiled Maidens of the Moon. To the Duke they bowed, and he to them. To Volkhavaar they bowed also. Volkhavaar did not bow; he nodded, most graciously.

The Duke spoke. The High Priest of the Sun spoke. Volkhavaar spoke.

After a while the priests and priestesses departed.

Overhead the sky was a swarthy blue; a great, shining cloud hid the sun. At noon, the god's chariot poised in that cloud, unseen, on the highest golden dome of the Temple, and gradually the cloud lost its light. Perhaps a storm was coming.

At sunset that day, the sun departed in muddy crimson flame. Evening closed in again like a black wolf pack.

Singing in Arkev then, holy, yet bizarre. Black cloaked priests passing along the wide thoroughfares, east and north, across the square, up a narrow street towards a grove of poplars at its summit. No one knew where these priests came from. From the Sun Temple, maybe, dressed differently to honor the one they sought. Or were they part of the retinue of Lord Volkhavaar? From their censers of blue-black metal came a sweet dragon's-breath of incense; but their music was different, baleful, an invocation of night.

The skies were heavy with cloud, starless, moonless now, as into the hidden garden the black priests went, and out of the hidden garden they returned. Down the narrow way they passed again, shadows thrown on walls, or possibly not shadows at all, only drifts of their own robes, the smoke of their censers. In their midst, something was carried.

Dogs ran out of their path, cats and rats slunk from it. Nightingales in wayside trees forgot their song. For some reason men did not venture abroad while the dark procession moved through the city, and few looked from windows.

The doors of the Sun Temple were open wide on the aureate glint and glimmer within.

Up brazen stairs and pearly stairs went the priests, in at the doors and the night seemed to follow them, eclipsing the brightness of the golden hall, the solar discs with their saffron rays, the fires—blazing once, now sinking—on the altar.

The priests of the idol—the demon-minions of Volkhavaar—set down the image in a small niche. A humble place it was, to the left of the great metallic things of the Sun, almost hidden. Yet, from that place, the dark continued to spread, like midnight ripples on a pool spreading from the fall of a stone. It grew cold there, also.

Priests of the Sun approached. Bowing, they welcomed him, Sovan Tovannazit, who was Takerna, the Black God. Polite they were, the sun priests, but only polite. No more. And quickly they hurried back to other duties when the brief ritual was completed, back to the light and warmth that felt oddly ephemeral now, in their sanctuary.

That night, Woana was not sleeping, not at all. She had learned that her wedding was to be in three days time. In the Temple of the Sun she and the Lord Volkhavaar were to be irrevocably joined in the sight of the gods. Her terror knew no limits, and her frenzied inner clamoring no answer. She considered flight but realized it was useless. Her father's soldiers and guards were everywhere; they would apprehend her, or he—Volkhavaar himself—might come after her, and then . . . Yes, she guessed his powers. Everyone guessed them it seemed, and no one would put a name to that guess. The ensorcelled city of Arkev understood in its bones the net it was under, yet was afraid to struggle for fear of other nets.

The hours of the dismal, moonless night, marked by the

temple bells, dragged their way over the inert body of the Duke's daughter.

At last she rose, and, wandering with a miserable aimlessness to the window, she threw open the pane and looked out. The dark was everywhere, impossible to pierce. And a fresh little needle stabbed at Woana. For the hundredth time, without hope, she called plaintively: "Mitz! Mitz! Come home."

And then, like a miracle, a sign that all would, despite everything, be well, Woana saw two sparks of green defy the night, and a slim, black shape evolve out of it, which, running on tiny, limber paws, sped from roof to roof and up and onto the sill.

"Mitz—oh, Mitz!" wept Woana, embracing her cat, covering her with kisses and tears.

Mitz, however, did not respond, as in the past, by snuggling close and purring. Rather, she seemed rigid in the Princess's grasp, and her fur bristled.

"Mitz, I'm so glad, oh, so glad to see you. Is it hungry you are? I have only a little milk here, but please take it. I daren't call for anything so late. I would fetch you something, but—oh, Mitz, I am afraid I might meet *him* if I went out of my room. Mitz, Mitz," her voice crouching small in her throat, "he is so dreadful. You fear him, too, don't you, my Mitz? That's why you wouldn't come back to me, why you keep so still now."

"Meearowoo," muttered Mitz, licking Woana's ear.

It was, after all, good to see Woana again, though bad, bad to be here. The will of the alien who had invaded Mitz's inner country had proved too strong to evade or resist. And now that will was a curious, inquiring intrusion, patently striving to comprehend this relationship between feline and human female that now suffused the cat's body.

Shaina's soul, unbearably confined and bruised and afraid, still marvelled at this rite of love, and tried also not to intrude, but could not help intruding, since things stood as they did.

It was not only the neighborhood of the magician that stifled Mitz's purr, but the ruffled embarrassment to which cats frequently fall prey.

Woana poured milk into a silver tray designed to contain brooches and Mitz lapped. Shaina at least was not revolted by this. Alas, the mouse they had caught—or rather the mouse Mitz had caught under great difficulty in Shaina's squeamish vicinity—had been left uneaten in the end, since Shaina could not force herself to stomach such fare. Growling, Mitz had stolen a half-burned sausage from a cook shop. This they had then devoured, though not entirely without problems either, since cats and humans eat dissimilarly, and several times both were nearly choked. Even now some of the milk was imbibed erroneously and presently sneezed back in many directions on the costly carpeting of the princess's bedroom.

Woana barely noticed, so glad she was to have her love again with her. Soon, sitting up in bed, Mitz in her arms, she recounted every scrap of the awful news and her ghastly destiny.

Shaina also heard. Her soul-heart went out to the anguished girl with her plain face and gentle affections. Mitz, however, her understanding limited to instinct and what she gleaned perforce through Shaina's grasp of human speech, would not be worried with it after her trying adventures. Almost wickedly, in the way of cats, she went voluntarily tumbling into immediate sleep like the putting out of a light, and Shaina, now subject to the natural laws of Mitz's body, was taken too.

After this, each confronted the other's fragmentary dreams. Shaina pursued mice and rolled in the sun, Mitz carried water from the well, was boxed on the ears soundly by old Ash's wife, and fell, over and over, in love with a handsome actor.

Through this medium of confusion, Shaina and Mitz were coming creditably to know each other, but Mitz's body jumped and spasmed on the pillows till dawn, by Woana's head. Woana, meanwhile, slept herself, some of the ink of terror washed from her by the cat's return. At least, until daybreak.

Three days was not long for a maid to prepare for her wedding. Never before had such a rush been known, nor such an unlikely hour for a wedding—midnight. But then who would have imagined so powerful a lord would have offered for graceless Woana: better snap him up quick. Besides, such wonderful gifts he produced for her trousseau. Three days they were coming into Arkev, black horses drawing lacquered wagons along the roads, black ships with purple sails moving, it seemed, without wind or use of oars, up the river Karga. Dresses for Woana of silk and velvet, and all armored with jewels, trinkets fit for the Moon Lady herself, perfumes from the Earth's four corners, black hunting dogs, black nightingales in silver cages.

Each day all this was marvelled at in the city, each day the palace stables were overflowing, and the halls and anterooms piled to the ceilings with riches. Each fresh dawn, all of it was mysteriously gone—stables empty, rooms empty, ready to receive new wagons and teams and new presents. No doubt the previous presents had been stored. No doubt. Volk, Master of Illusion, Kernik, Stealer of Scenes.

The Duchess simpered. The Duke sweated and looked over his shoulder. He had begun to be oppressed by things that were not there—swarms of bees he swatted at, plagues of fleas he crushed between agitated nails. Woana, unlovely-pale as soaked bread, ran ropes of pearls through her fingers, and thanked her husband-to-be. The pearls did not seem as real as Volkhavaar. Nothing did.

"Come, timid maiden," said he, strolling with her in the gardens. "Do you suppose I will eat you?" And he smiled unreassuringly, seeing quite clearly in her flickering gaze that she would not be at all surprised if he did.

As for Mitz and her fellow traveller, they were growing closer, not in love, but in the ways of twinship. Mitz snapped up a dragonfly: Shaina stifled retching and kept silent. Shaina made Mitz pursue the magician as he walked; Mitz suffered it. Volkhavaar saw Mitz. He bowed to her. Volkhavaar was partial to cats.

Dasyel came by, walking after the magician. Dasyel sat still, near to the magician. Shaina moved Mitz to jump onto the bench beside him, to sit leaning on his ribs. Dasyel never noticed.

Shaina's soul-heart melted with pity and loss. Mitz, unnerved, began to wash her face.

The three days passed, and were gone.

It was the morning of the wedding, the afternoon, the evening of the wedding.

Woana, in a dress of gold, was praying. It was all that was left to her.

All over the city, the streets were hung with ribbons and flowers. As the night drew on, cloudy as all the nights had been since Volkhavaar had come, fireworks provided stars for the sky, and the fountains already ran like blood with wine, and oxen roasted on vast spits in the Great Square.

Woana was still praying.

Then the Lord came riding in his purple finery on his jet-colored horse, a crown like an emperor's on his head. His retinue was composed of a thousand, so it seemed. Soldiers in black and gold, maidens in lilac and azure who danced and cast glitter from baskets of roses. Chariots shaped like swans that seemed to fly, amber doves that circled overhead, musicians with instruments of one or many strings, pipes and drums, bears the shade of a wheat field, with collars of sapphire. How the crowd roared.

And then the trumpets, and the palace doors thrown open.

She wore a veil of tinsel, but it could not disguise or magnify her, the Plain Princess. She fumbled, and stumbled on the vast stairway. But Volkhavaar lifted her up onto one of his horses, grinning, as if she were the best of prizes. She had stopped praying now.

Almost the appointed hour, almost midnight. Torches scarlet and sky ebony. Did some perhaps puzzle, vaguely recollecting that, not so long since, midnight had been the appointed hour for some other dark and tremendous revelry?

Then the bells from the towers, the bells from the ships, and up the steps of the Sun Temple, Volkhavaar led his betrothed, his eyes like adders, exalting in the whole colossal joke.

Into the Temple passed the bridal procession, Volkhavaar, and Woana on his arm like a wisp of paper born along on a flood tide, the sinister retinue, the Duke and Duchess, the court, the guards.

The priests were waiting at the burnished altar.

Volkhavaar strode to it, pulling Woana with him.

Then a great lull, the cessation of movement. The bridegroom halted some way from the altar. The bridegroom let go the hand of his intended. And now, a great stillness, as if silence had been poured into that place from an enormous urn. And then the voice of Volkhavaar.

"No, sir priests. One moment, if you please."

An interim followed. Whispers, falling off. Shortly, Volkhavaar's voice once more, yet different, less playful, less civilized. A savage voice, belonging to a slave above a quarry, a boy on a rock.

"Black Lord, High Lord, Wind Lord, Lord of Night and Shadowed Places. *They* forgot, but your servant does not. I am your true priest. You know me. I am your son. O, Sovan Tovannazit of the ruined shrine, look about at your new lodging. Remember the descent from the mountain, the smashing of your power and mine. Remember the ill days, the petty crimes, the foul dungeon, the slave who must die hewing white stone for Arkev. Remember the man who mocked us both. Remember how I spilled my life on your stone, how I rose, and you with me, falcon in the sky. Rise now, Illimitable One. O Sovan Tovannazit, come. Come and possess. O Sovan, Eater of Shadows, O Takerna, O TAKERNA TAKERNA—TAKERNA COME AND POSSESS!"

There was a noise, above, below—everywhere. It was heard throughout Arkev, and further. The sky seemed split, the earth seemed dismantled. The Temple was splashed by screams, imprecations and groans. Every light was extinguished. Yet somehow a lightless brilliance persisted, and grew.

It was the color of a black sun shining through a pane of black crystal. It had no business to be, but it was.

Its source, from which it emanated and spread, was a niche to the left of the High Altar. Something was standing in the niche, small and dark: the idol from the shrine.

Even the priests made no move as they watched beneath the deadened gold of the solar discs. From four sides of the Temple, eyes staring, breaths held, mouths dry with the acid of fear.

Not in the cramping niche, but before it, between the altar and the spot where the purple lord was waiting, his arms uplifted, a burning shadow was soaring up, coming to the height his arms described, surpassing them.

The Black God.

Face of a terrible bird, hook of nose, blind seeing malice of eyes alert for prey, mouth made of a curse. In one hand the offering horn clasped close, an empty horn, ready for blood. Shapes like black lightnings, daggers, swords, depended from a belt like a curling serpent.

From whichever side of the Temple they stared, this they saw, the priests and the court of Arkev city, for east, west, north and south there was a countenance, a hand, a hungry horn. You could not get behind the back of Sovan Tovannazit the four-faced, he could see every way.

The god grew until his head touched the tall ceiling. Then he was still, a pillar like ebony or iron, but neither, a thing without a mote of color or beauty, and iridescent with untraceable light.

Takerna. Takerna made mighty.

Volkhavaar snapped his fingers. A wild, barbaric music started up. It covered the Temple as the inky glare covered it.

Above, in the towers, the bells began to ring discordantly, and presently, all over the city, bells were jangling out of tune.

Volkhavaar looked about.

"Kneel," he said. "Kneel to the Lord you have neglected. Marble for the palace, gold for the sun, silver for the moon and stars. For him, nothing. Kneel and beg his pardon, kneel and entreat him."

And to a man, to a woman, the Duke's court, even the priests, found that they had obeyed, had obeised themselves, and a guttural cringing whimper crawled from their throats.

Only Volkhavaar and his demons were upright now before the god.

"Come," Volk said to his bride, pulling her up also, "we are to be married."

Three black, fettered goats had been driven in and along the aisle between the kneeling, cowering ranks. Volk took them by the horns, one by one, and with a silver knife he slashed their throats, red blood falling black on the black feet of the god. At each choked animal scream, an answering scream all around. Blood formed black, slender rivers on the mosaic floor. In that liquor Volk dipped his finger. He held Woana as pitilessly as he had held the goats, by her hair, and on her forehead he set a mark of blood and on her thin, little breast. Her eyes bulged; she did not resist. When he let her go she stood like all the rest, as if turned to stone.

Volk glanced about, to the place where the priests were crowded.

"Now you serve Sovan Tovannazit, your mysteries and your symbols shall be different."

He made over them a sign in the air, and their scarlet and their yellow metal were gone. Black now, the priests of Volk, the acolytes of the Black God.

They got up like sleepwalkers. They began to dance to

the music. Out of their censers smoked a drug that filled the hall with its fragrance; from their sprinklers of holy water fell drops of blood. All the Temple now was coming to its feet, eyes fixed, hands reaching for hands, the dance overtaking them.

"Come, my wife, my father, my mother," said Volkhavaar.

He went to the Temple doors, Woana moving stiff as wood beside him, the Duke and the Duchess moving after with carved smiles and eyes like buttons.

The huge crowd of people clustered in the Sun Court, not feasting, not festive; silent, gazing at the black-blazing Temple in wonder and alarm. All Arkev was quiet, yet, as before, in its bones, Arkev knew.

Volk lifted his hand with Woana's hand held in it. Trumpets sounded. Not from the trumpeters' lips, but out of the sky, and the bells went on and discordantly on.

No one cheered, no hats were thrown or coins, no pigeons flew in a cloud. Only the strange music came spilling from the Temple, and the priests in their new sables, and, like a dance of the dead, a corpse-dance, a possession by dancing demons, the crowd in the Court began to stamp and circle, and, in a huge wheel, turned out of the Court and through the streets. And somehow the music went with them, so that soon, under the inpenetrable sky, the whole city danced to honor Sovan Tovannazit, the god it had forgotten.

Until, inevitably, the dance altered, took on another aspect, also barbaric, also of the shadows.

In the Temple of the Sun, on the High Altar there, a black horse was dancing on its hind limbs, defiling with its dung the sacred vessels and the holy cloth. In the body of the Temple the dance of lust had seized them too. Not only man with woman; other things. Shapes like bulls, shapes like wolves, and white girls lying down with them. Men mounting mares. Cries of pain and ecstasy, and birds beating their wings.

The priests from the Star Temple ran naked in the thoroughfares hunting rats, roasting their catch on fires, or eating it raw. The Moon Maidens screamed shrill as devils, rent their veils, and were presently maidens no longer. Fireless smokes were rising, and lightnings striking haphazardly, like arrows, claiming several in the acts of love or hate, scorching the tops of towers.

Miles from Arkev, east and north, in the villages and towns, even as far as the Volkyan Plain, people left their beds to stare at the sky west and south of the Korkeem. They asked each other in nervous voices what such lights and thunderings in heaven could mean, hoping no one would answer.

✳ 19 ✳

The black feast of Takerna.

As a boy, Kernik, with his god, had held sway over an entire village. That had been triumph, then. Now they tasted Arkev on their tongue, Volk's tongue, Takerna's tongue.

The orgy was at its indescribable height when the magician and his bride returned to the Duke's palace. Of the Duke and the Duchess there was no sign.

Within doors. The dim fires and exhalations, the moans and cries and shrieks shut out behind the colored windows. The demon-people had evaporated, and no human servants or guards remained. Volk and his wife had the palace to themselves.

Volk looked at her, and she, blank-faced, backed a step, backed a step, away from him.

"I see my fish-skin Duchess is in terror that I am about to demand my conjugal rights of her. Well, madam, no need to quake. You can keep your milk-and-water maidenhead. Such things don't interest me. Even if you were beautiful, I should not be interested. I leave that pastime to the beasts of the field, and the other sort of beasts who dwell in houses."

Woana tremblingly collapsed upon a chair.

Volk stood by a window, intent, his profile so very like that other profile, Takerna's.

"No, ugly little girl," said Volkhavaar, musingly, "all I want from you is your symbolic value. Magicians must deal in symbols, and so symbols become dear to them, and especially to me. Lord of Magicians, High Priest of all symbols. When your unfortunate parents are no longer with us, which will be soon enough, you will inherit the Korkeem, and I, your husband, will rule it. Otherwise, you may do as you please, so long as you do not inconvenience me. Now you can run along, indeed you can, to your narrow virginal bed."

Woana somehow got herself erect, out of the room and up the stairways of the silent, deserted palace. Shuddering with relief and horror she sidled into her bedchamber and bolted and barred the door—that useless and unneeded precaution she had practised before.

Even here, she felt his eyes on her, watching her. She did not doubt he could see through walls if he wished.

Outside, the frenzied noises continued.

Woana got into bed and pulled the covers over her ears. She wanted to sponge the mark of blood from her, but she did not, for some reason, dare to. She had called Mitz, but Mitz had not replied; probably Mitz was in hiding again, as Woana fervently longed to be herself. What had he said about her father and her mother? She could not recall, perhaps was afraid to. She did not love them, but to imagine them at the mercy of Volkhavaar—oh, she pitied them. And she was helpless.

Surely it must be dawn soon? How she ached for the morning.

Four or five hours from midnight the sun should have risen over Arkev. But the sun did not rise. Sunless, moonless, starless, the sky continued black above the domes and spires. The god of night had put out all lights but his own.

The other flames were sinking into exhaustion now, and quiet. Sleepers were intermingled on the streets. Only old smoke drifted through the gardens and the porticos.

Like dead fish cast up by a retreating tide of violence, Takerna's worshippers sprawled about his feet in the temple which was now his, among the blood and wine.

But the god was not sleeping, the god never slept, once he had been woken.

Pad, pad, pad. Lupine claws on the floor. A black wolf, tall as a horse, came through the doorway, up the aisle, delicately stepping over those who lay there. On the muzzle of the wolf something sticky, and out in the streets some who would be sleeping forever, with red necklaces. The shepherd who was also the wolf had been plundering his flock in the cold hour of dawn when no sun rose.

The Duke and Duchess of the Korkeem awoke as one and stared as one at the wolf. Then the wolf was gone, and it was Volkhavaar who stood there, their dear son-in-law.

"How odd," remarked the Duchess in a dazed uncertain twitter. "What are all these chains doing?"

"Binding you to the pillar," said Volkhavaar. "Or maybe it is only an illusion. Try them and see."

"Why, what a novel thing. Is it some custom of the Volkyan?"

"Now it is," said Volk.

"I demand to be released," blustered the Duke, staring about, at chains, at pillar, at all the dire and hellish confusion; somehow omitting to stare at the tall shadow whose head touched the ceiling.

"Presently you shall be," said Volk. "First, are there words you wish to say to me, some last request or blessing, or even some curse?"

The Duchess's face contorted.

"Clemency!" she cried. "I will do anything, only spare me!"

"I have everything I want."

"Guard!" shouted the Duke, "Help! Help!"

"No guard, no help. No longer are you needful, sir and lady. Even my master does not want your niggling little souls."

"He is a wolf!" shrilled the Duchess. "I saw! I saw!"

Volk stretched his mouth. He bowed and kissed the hem of the robe of the immense, dark idol.

Do you recall the priest called Voy? Yes, Incredible One, you do. How many times already in this long night has your lightning calcined domes and men alike, in the streets of this, your city. Now, like the industrious woman, there is this last bit of dirt we must sweep out of the house." Volk stepped aside. He observed the Duke and Duchess—laboring the stone for whose white-towered palace he should, in a quarry, have died—and both their faces were white and crumbling as that stone. "Take them, my lord and master," said Volkhavaar.

And the roaring came, and the black brightness, and the aroma of charred flesh, and there by the pillar stood two torches, one about the height of Duke Moyko, one about the height of Duke Moyko's wife.

Cats have sundials in their heads. They know which hour it is, no matter what. Mitz knew it was dawn, and past dawn, even as she crouched in the hollow bole of the oak in the palace garden. Even when she put out her head and saw the city still black from end to end with the deepest midnight.

"The golden sky-eye has refused to open," thought Mitz.

"No," replied Shaina, staring through Mitz's eyes, "the sun has risen. But Volkhavaar has drawn a black canopy of illusion and cloud over Arkev, so no one can see the sun-chariot."

"Maybe you are right," said Mitz, "but I am going in again to hide."

"No, you are not," said Shaina, "Are you not hungry? Let us go into the great kitchen and see what's to be had."

By this means Shaina persuaded her hostess out of the tree where they had taken refuge at the first peal of sorcerous thunder. But the leap from oak to lawn was not a great success.

"Almost in the pool you had us," chided Mitz.

"Listen," said Shaina, "you with your sharp ears—can you even hear a mouse squeaking?"

Mitz and Shaina, prowling through the grasses, came up the mossy path, and there the palace lay.

Mitz flattened down to her belly, and her fur rose, Shaina's tail—yes, she thought of it as her property too, now—expanded like a broom-head, and they growled with one common emotion.

No longer was the palace of Arkev white, no longer were the domes of pale and glimmering gold, no longer the windows of rose and hyacinth and sea-green glass. *Oh* no. Black the palace was, iron the domes, grey and purple and ominous dragon's-blood the windows. And now look about, and see how every tree in the garden bears black leaves, how all the flowers are the color of poison and the lawns like powdered charcoal. Look at Arkev, the Always-Bright. Black walls, black spires, nothing shining; one great necropolis under Takerna's sky.

Mitz scaled the black tower. Noiseless birds huddled in the eaves. In at the altered windows of Woana's room Mitz and Shaina looked.

"She's sleeping. He hasn't harmed or defiled her," said Shaina.

Mitz spat. She scratched at the pane, but Woana did not wake. Mitz fled.

"Wait!" cried Shaina's soul, swept up physically and mentally also by the cat's wild panic. Down the tower into a slender tree, tree to tree, down in grass, through a small hole, up steps, over a wall, into a great wide street paved from a tar barrel, where one torch still burned with an unwholesome sepia flame. "Wait."

"No wait—" Mitz's cry—"Night! Fear! Flight!"

Shaina, all cold in the hot spiky forest of Mitz's fright, held to her sanity precariously. "All right, Mitz, nice Mitz, pretty Mitz, go like the wind, follow the clouds. Good to run, fine to run. But if you are running, let us run *this* way."

And so they did, taking the direction in which Shaina knew the Temple lay, not because she wished to see its ruin, but because she sensed Dasyel was there. And also because—she could not quite say.

It was a curious uncomfortable volatile thing which was happening to Shaina. Caught in the mill-race of Mitz's feline terror, she felt old, primitive fibers interweave in her own spirit. Always sensitive, part witch, as Barbayat had said, now her transplanted soul had become almost unbearably receptive. The sorcery and the night slashed and devilled her, yet she felt on the brink of—what? 'Don't ask now,' Shaina thought, 'don't try to reason. Not yet.'

And then they were at the Sun Temple doors, before Mitz had even realized.

"Too late to turn back," said Shaina to Mitz.

"I will claw you and gnaw you," grated Mitz.

"Kind Mitz, gentle Mitz. No one will hurt you."

"I will hurt *you*," promised Mitz. "I will pounce and play with you, and nibble you and crush your backbone with my paw. I—"

Shaina lost patience. "I will make you bite your own tail," said she, "if you don't hold your tongue."

Mitz grew silent, and the fur lay down on her and Shaina's back. Shaina, quick pupil of Barbayat's teaching, was after all the stronger.

The Temple had an underwater appearance, steeped in shade and littered with its orgiastic detritus. And there were two strange heaps of ashes on the floor. But what was that tall thing, that pitchy thing, that—

Mitz did not want to, Shaina did not either, but somehow they stole forward, very close, and right up into that face they looked, that falcon-demon face of Sovan Tovannazit-Takerna.

Then someone spoke. Not the idol. The magician's voice saying extraordinary things:

"Here, pussy, pussy. Come sit on the knee of the Duke of the Korkeem, come share his throne with him. These are the hours of Volkhavaar's triumph."

And suddenly there was a mouse on the mosaic, scuttling busily. Or rather, it was the illusion of a mouse. Shaina darkened her thoughts and steeled herself. Mitz, instinct uppermost, ran a little, sprang, toyed and horribly patted and mangled. Each motion took her a fraction nearer the magician, as he meant it to. At last, hunger getting the better of her, Mitz slew and devoured the unreal mouse. Real enough it tasted.

Shaina emerged from hiding, ignored the warm afterglow of mouse-gore in Mitz's throat, and found they were seated on the magician's knees.

"You shall have a proper breakfast later," he said, looking down at the cat with his paper dehumanized face and leaden eyes. "Little, cruel, clever, wicked one. You think you are satisfied, but that was only a dream you fed on."

Mitz, oddly moved and embarrassed, commenced washing her paws. Shaina kept herself in the background, and caught glimpses of things obliquely as Mitz turned her head.

The chair was gold and black, the Duke's chair, or the High Priest's, or an amalgam of both; in any case, much finer. Yevdora, the lovely zombie-daughter, seated to his left, spinning smoke with a golden wheel and silver distaff. To his right, Dasyel, reading aloud from a book all emeralds. Nearby, Roshi in the form of a bear, playing a pipe of jade. Symbols. For the magician, as he said, loved symbols, needed them; the foundations of his house.

"Little black cat," said Volk, soft and dry, "I have made bright, beautiful Arkev dark and ugly. I have made my god, Arkev's god, see, there he is. I have drunk the hot blood of men."

And then his hands came with a light smooth touch and stroked Mitz end to end.

Mitz's eyes shut. She purred. She discovered the purr, stopped it. Began to purr again. Who would have thought the purple man would have such a caress?

Shaina felt the caress also, marvelled at it. Almost it made her forget, but not quite. . . .

The idol, Shaina. Remember that.

Yes. She recognized the idol, Volk's black god. It was the little demon-deity of the mountain village, the changeable one the goats feared, the angry one she had bowed to and placated with a flower.

Mitz purred and slept, and Shaina was pulled down after her, purring and sleeping.

Black falcons were flying. The air was full of their wings.

Soon the word was running. There is a new Duke in Arkev. The old Duke's daughter is his wife. His name is Volkhavaar. And he is saying that from every town and city, every village and farm, and from the temples too, a tribute must be sent him. Forty black oxen, a hundred black sheep, two hundred black cattle; fifty barrels of black beer, sixty of red wine, a ton of silver, a ton of gold, six caskets of diamonds, the fur of twenty black bears, the fleece of eighty black rams.

There were other things, stories. How Arkev was held under a cloud of perpetual night. How Volkhavaar had banished the old religion, and the sun, the moon and the stars had deserted the city. How all the priests now served a cruel god of lust and blood, and the Maidens were whores and worse. How the caravans and the ships which had gone to Arkev for the Spring Fair had none of them come back along the road.

Some refused to send the gifts their Duke required. Odd, how the lightning forked here and there, and here and there a prince went up in smoke.

All the Korkeem knew his name at last, Volk Volkhavaar, and the ways were packed with treasure and herds hurrying to Arkev the No Longer Bright, the no longer sky-worshipping city.

The red sun priest was riding back to Kost along the rough track that led over the hill from Old Ash's village.

It was early, not long after sun-up, the mountains still dark on the enamelled luster of the sky; the air was silver with the sound of cow bells, the song of birds, and the belly of the portly priest well-lined. Nevertheless, riding on his mule, he was far from light or comfortable of heart.

True, he had done his best for the valley. And a gruelling hard best had been demanded of him. What could you do about a vampire but what he had done? Better for her, and the only answer for this village and the other villages also hereabouts. Yet somehow, he did not feel right

about it, had had to force himself to the necessary act.
Smiting off her head was a dreadful task enough, but it
had seemed to him her voice was beating all around him
as he did it, like a frenzied bird, and when the blow was
accomplished and they trudged homewards, down from
the grave, was it weeping he heard, soft as rain on the
wind behind him? The stroke of the sword brought peace,
even to the undead, so he knew. But to that one maiden,
was it peace?

Now, of course, his return journey to Kost was taking
him past the graveyard, and presently very close to the
spot where the slave lay buried. And, broad daylight or
not, well-versed and intelligent or not, he would be glad
when the hill was behind him, and there was no denying
it.

The mule, at no time a great lover of journeys, had
been plodding along in a forbearing and self-righteous
fashion. Now, all at once, it stopped.

"Come, giddy-up, my fat friend," said the priest.

The mule shook its head.

The priest noticed then that a small boulder, which
must have rolled down from higher up, had lodged itself
in the middle of the track.

"It's a stone you're afraid of now, is it?"

Just at that moment the boulder gave a sort of shift
and a lift—or seemed to. The mule let out a noise like
gravel blown vigorously through the wrong end of a
trumpet, and took three wild leaps, to the west, to the east,
and backwards. This last unseated the priest, who fell with
a thud in the dust.

"Praise the Sun-King I am well-cushioned for such
events," grunted the priest philosophically, getting up.

"So he is," said another voice. "I am glad. I shouldn't
like to see the good father bruised."

"I say nothing of bruises," amended the priest, "though
my bones are intact." And his sharp eyes went up and
over the old woman who stood there on the track, observing him. A strange, grey-looking old woman she was, in a
bundle of mossy shawl, and with eyes at least as sharp as
his own.

"Mules are silly creatures," said the old woman, "quiet
one minute, skittish the next. See, one of the bundles fell
too, but I have put it back."

"My thanks," said the priest. "And may I know who I am thanking?"

"Only a poor old lady from the mountains hereabouts," said the grey woman. "But tell me, has the good father heard the news from Arkev?"

"Something I heard. A new Duke with new ways."

"Worse than that. Look to your red robe and your golden sun disc, father; someone doesn't care for such things."

"Advice given on the road should always be listened to," said the priest. "But still I should like to know how the wise lady is called."

" 'Tell me your name, it will make all the difference between us,' " remarked the old woman, "as the dog said to the flea. And there goes the father's mule at a fast trot. I am thinking maybe he had better make after the animal, unless he would rather be walking to Kost."

The priest, knowing quite well what he was up against, gave the witch a curt nod and set off after the mule, which had kicked up its heels and broken into one of those debonair, yet brief, canters to which its kind were subject.

Sure enough, about half a mile down the other side of the hill, the mule stopped running to engage in mock battle with a young fir tree, and the priest was presently returned to its back. "But I shall be visiting you later, perhaps, mother," thought he to himself.

It was not until noon, when he paused to eat his midday fare, that the priest thought to inspect the bundle the witch had put her fingers on. Then there were a few words spoken, and not all holy ones.

The sacred bronze sword from the temple at Kost, the blessed sword for the slaying of vampires, was gone.

But the priest would have been even more angry and alarmed had he turned aside from the track over the hill that day, and seen what had been done to the grave of Old Ash's slave.

* 20 *

Inside a windowless, mossy-boulder house, inside a round, closed door, lit by the candles burning in a chandelier of human-skulls, sat the witch, staring in her crystal. She saw this:

A black city under a black sky in which a sun burned cold and pale as phosphorous. A jet-stone Temple with a black flame leaping. Priests clothed in sable bowing to a great image with a nightmare face. Black mares prancing and copulating on the altar, and the blood of beasts and men a scarlet rain. A jet-stone palace stood close by, where a dark Duke sat on a golden throne with a little, wan Duchess at his side. A yellow haired girl was spinning smoke, a blond bear danced, a young man gazed from blind, sea eyes. Before the Duke, kneeling, princes and lords extended caskets of jewels and coins. Ships on the river, caravans on the roads. Up on a roof, a small cat eating a fish head. A cat's brain thinking of the stroking hand of a magician; a girl's soul perched in that brain like a bird on a windy and uncertain bough.

Enough looking, even for Barbayat.

So round Barbayat turned, and there on the floor was a symbol drawn in white clay—a symbol never before drawn there. And just outside the symbol, something wrapped in grey cloth, which was shaped like a life-size doll. And inside the symbol, standing point down in the ground, hilt uppermost, a sword of bronze.

"Well now, Sword," said Barbayat. "I will tell you. Someone is lying dead, there, in that cloth quite near you. A young maiden, whose head you smote off, did you not? Well, now, Sword, answer me, by the power of the clay that holds you, and the power of the fire that tempered you, and the power of the water that cooled you, and the power of the air which you cleave with a stroke, and the power of the earth in which you stand. Answer, Sword, for answer I will have."

The Sword spoke. It had, fittingly, a brassy voice.

"Yes," rang the Sword.

"Listen to me," said Barbayat. "Do you know me for a witch?"

"Yes," rang the Sword.

"My name is Barbayat, Sword. Tell me my name."

"Barbayat," rang the Sword. "Greetings, Barbayat."

"Now I name you. I name you Sword. I name you Bronze. Listen, Sword of Bronze. There lies the maiden whose head you smote off. Did you smite off her head?"

"Yes, Barbayat."

"Listen, Sword, I tricked her, but her blood's in my veins, and the trick weighs like lumps in the porridge. I and she have kept her soul in this world. So, know this, Sword: what Is, is, what Was, was, but what is To Be, may be otherwise. You smote off her head?"

"Yes, Barbayat."

"Three times you have answered "yes" to that question, Sword, but soon you shall answer differently. This is the oldest magic: what we *believe* Is, what we *believe* Was, and what is To Be *will* be. Now you believe you slew the maiden. When you forget you slew the maiden, when you answer "no" more times than you have answered "yes", you will change the past as all who remember and unremember things change it, and then it will not have been. When you, who took her life, tell me you did not take it, and *believe* you did not take it, it will not have been taken, and the maiden's body will be whole again. And her soul, since it lingers on this earth, can reclaim it, and she will live. Do you understand?"

"I understand, Barbayat. But I know the stroke I made in the priest's hands, the warmth of her blood, and the severing. *Still*, I know."

Barbayat only nodded.

"Sword, I named you Bronze. But bronze is two metals; copper and tin. Sword, I name you again. I name you Copper, and I name you Tin. Answer me now, Copper, warm, red Copper, metal of flame from a warm, near land. Answer me now, Tin, cold, grey tin, metal of cinders from a cold, far land."

The sword seemed to shudder the length of itself; it grew strangely and inconclusively mottled, a mottling of fire and ash, running together, drawing apart, fluid as in its molten state.

"Greetings, Barbayat," sang the deep, hot voice of Copper.

"Greetings, Barbayat," shrilled the thin, chilly voice of Tin.

"Tell me, Copper of the sword, have you slain a maiden recently?" asked Barbayat.

"I was forged to slay," replied the Copper. "I am strong and hungry. No doubt I slew."

"Tell me, Tin of the sword, have you also slain a maiden."

"I? I am flimsy and delicate I should like to nick and bite. I may have scratched her, but I doubt I slew her."

"Fool!" roared the Copper. "With me beside you, you could slay a hundred men; one maiden would be easy for us. Take my hand and recollect—the jar of bone, the taste of blood."

"Yes," whined the Tin, "maybe I do, maybe I did. Yes. With my brother's help, I slew the maiden."

Barbayat only nodded.

"Sword, I named you Bronze; Bronze, I named you Copper and Tin. I will name you again. Back on the anvil they hammered you, before the anvil, in the furnace, they mixed you, and before they mixed you, smelted and melted you." Inside the shape of clay the sword seemed to dissolve, to run apart, the copper with an angry mutter, the tin with a wild shriek. "Ingot of Tin I name you, Ingot of Copper I name you. Tell me," said Barbayat, "Ingot of Tin, where did they find you sleeping?"

The voice of Tin came softly now, dreamily and distantly, as if across great seas and wilderness.

"Deep I lay, Barbayat, in my burrow of rock. Who told me what I was? None. I was a part of my Mother, the earth. Cool and long I slept, till men ripped me from my mother's breast. Black and secret I was, but over water they took me and burned me in fire and poured me out and bound me with a fierce, red other who hated me, and hammered me cruelly, and my spirit was altered."

"Return," said the witch, "to what you were."

And the Tin ran away into a dull darkness on the floor.

"Tell me," said Barbayat, "Ingot of Copper, where did they find *you* sleeping?"

The voice of the Copper was also changed; mellow it came, with many different notes to it.

"Many of us there were, Barbayat, a colony, a family,

set like a fern on one stem. Deep we lay, and chattered to each other and loved each other. Who told us what we were? We did. Who told us what we should become? We. But we were wrong. Men ripped us apart. They ground us in a pestle and broke us in pieces. They put us in fire till we wept, and then bound us with a cold, grey other who hated us, and we were no more All but only One. The hammer was cruel, but not so cruel as that separation and that awful joining."

"Return," said the witch, "to what you were."

And the copper scattered and then amalgamated in a ruddy clustering on the floor.

"And now," said Barbayat, "I will name you for the last time: Oxide of Copper, Oxide of Tin."

"Greetings, Barbayat," whispered one.

"Greetings, Barbayat," murmured another.

"Well, now, I will tell you," said the witch. "Someone is lying dead, there, in that cloth quite near you. A young maiden, whose head you smote off, did you not?"

"I?" cried the whisper. "No, Barbayat, I know only secrecy, not death."

"I?" cried the murmur. "No, Barbayat, I know only companionship, not death."

"Be sure," said Barbayat, "remember the blessing at Kost, the priest's hands, the jar of bone, the taste of blood. Did you smite off the maiden's head?"

"No, Barbayat."

"No, Barbayat."

"Earth," said Barbayat, "fire, air and water. The mining, the furnace, the mixing, the hammer on the anvil, the cooking. Oxide be Tin, be Copper. Tin and Copper be one, be Bronze. Bronze be Sword." And on the ground the dust swirled and the red and the grey came together and mingled, and there stood the burnished, holy sword, point down, hilt uppermost.

"Sword," said Barbayat, "I have made you again. You are new and unstained, virgin and innocent. Listen, Sword of Bronze. There lies the maiden whose head you smote off. Did you smite off her head?"

"No, Barbayat," rang the sword in its proud, bright voice. "No, and no, and no."

And the witch gave a laugh like a fox's bark and, turning about, whipped the cloth from the doll-like shape lying just outside the clay-drawn symbol.

And there lay Shaina on her own midnight hair, still as if sleeping, serene as grace, and her head joined firmly and cream-smooth to her neck and her neck to her slender shoulders, and never even a scar to say otherwise. While from her body, barely visible, there rose like a slim and sparkling smoke, a silver chain. Unbroken.

Just before sunrise, someone came walking from Cold Crag, crossed over the rock bridge, and on to the track that led down the grassy mountain with its goat pasture and streams, towards the hills and the valley below.

Someone looked just like a village woman, strong shoes, apron, kerchief over grey hair and a mossy shawl. Someone was leading a little mule and cart, and in the cart was a plain, sad, wooden box that could be nothing but a coffin. A melancholy sight, an unlucky sight. Presently, when the village woman and her dismal burden had gone over the hill and were on the hard wide road to Kost, and beyond it, people would take off their caps, get out of the way, offer a slice of bread or an apple. Which would all be very useful to Barbayat who, having a maiden's newly repaired body to take care of, could travel in no other fashion.

However, before she was quite off the mountain track, Barbayat took time to notice one small thing.

The carved idol which had stood in the rock side near the bottom of the track for so many uncountable years, seemed at first glance to have vanished, so thick were the white flowers growing round it.

The Grey Lady went close. She peered and poked, nodding to the idol politely the while. Hard to read her boulder-stony face, but before she went on, a flower or two she picked and placed them on the wooden box in the cart.

✳ 21 ✳

Shaina was dreaming she had caught a mouse and was playing with it on the mosaic floor of the palace. This was Mitz's cat dream; Shaina was in a manner used to it, so that a surrealistic grimness overhung the fantasy. Then the nature of the dream changed. No longer was the mouse in Shaina's jaws; Shaina had become the mouse. Out of the cat's hot, wet, armored mouth she fell, close by another mouse—a mouse she somehow knew to be Dasyel. "Run!" she squeaked, "Volk the cat is after us," but the mouse-Dasyel only looked at her with beautiful apathetic blue-green eyes, and then Volk's paw descended on both their backs with the pain of fire and the weight of iron.

Shaina awoke with a horrible start, and promptly fell off some high place into some other, lower place. This had frequently happened to her when her dreams and the dreams of Mitz became entangled.

"I beg your pardon," signalled Shaina to Mitz, sat up and began to wash her paws, and—

No longer black-furred and narrow, but brown and smooth and narrow, with ten familiar fingers. No, not true. Still a dream. Impossible.

Shaina shut her eyes, opened them. She was seeing differently, hearing differently. No use trying to run along on four feet, and, Mother-Earth-be-kind, she had almost broken her back just then, attempting to turn in the way of cats right over her own spine.

"Shaina, you are mad. Collect your wits," said Shaina. For now she was standing upright, a wind blowing about in her hair, and even, yes, talking to herself in a well remembered voice. "What has happened to me?"

And then she noticed a hillside, a stormy sky, a cart with an open box in it . . . and sitting up in the cart, wrapped in her shawl, the witch from Cold Crag.

"Barbayat," said Shaina—very slowly, with the tears hurting in her eyes, and the terror and joy waiting side by

174

side in her heart, each ready to flood through her—"Barbayat, tell me everything, at once, and quickly."

So Barbayat, Grey Lady, told her, quick as a wink but with little left out.

Then Shaina meowed—she could not help it—and tried to leap after a dragonfly for pure, crazy delight—and then recollected all that was done with, and touched every part of herself to make sure all of her was there. She could not believe it, even so, and thanked Barbayat as an empress would have thanked a goddess, and then suddenly sat down on the hillside and laughed and wept her heart out of her breast.

Barbayat waited a while, and then she said:

"Time enough for crying later, maybe. I told you how I took you from your grave and made you whole again and drew you home to your own flesh. Now, my daughter, that is the settling of an account between us. Once I deceived you but I have paid my debt. Say I have paid it."

"A hundred times over, Barbayat; paid, paid and paid."

"Good. Then, if I am mentioning to you other things and you are acting on them in your own wild way and the net catches you again; maiden, you no longer have a claim on me for rescue. Let that be understood."

"Yes, Barbayat. What things?"

"What things. Ah, what things. Here are apples and here is a loaf. Eat, while you listen. First, I will say this. The door is still open, my round door. Come back with me to my mountain, and I will make a witch of you sure as a bee makes honey. Then we shall see some things done. Yes, you are shaking your head, as I knew. The spirit and the heart remain the same. He comes before all else, your Dasyel. Well, then. Swallow the apple before you choke on it, and tell me what you learned when you ran on four feet in Arkev under Volk's sable sky."

Shaina obeyed—between trying to remonstrate with Barbayat and trying to remember not to eat as a cat does, she had indeed been near enough to choking.

"I learned the byways of the city and the byways of the palace. I learned how to catch mice—which lesson I do not cherish, as the Grey Lady may understand—I learned the rites of the magician's black god and witnessed them. I learned that the magician has a gentle touch for the back of a cat."

Barbayat sat like a boulder in the cart beside the open

coffin, and she looked northwards over the hill slope at a range of black mountains, which were really all one great canopy of storm.

"Anything else?"

"One thing else," said Shaina, "one thing that rang inside me like a bell. I don't know why. I learned that Volk's god, the god he has made king in Arkev, is the same god as that small gentleman to whom I bowed on the mountain."

"And did you," said Barbayat, "at any time offer to that gentleman on the mountain?"

"Once, when he looked angry, and my heart was heavy, I offered him a white flower."

"So it seemed. There is a bush of white flowers growing there now," said Barbayat.

Then Barbayat pointed where she looked, northwards, at the black storm mountains that smothered the horizon.

"There lies Arkev," said she, "Arkev in Volkhavaar's night. One day only, will it take a resolute young maiden to reach that place on her two feet. But it is a dark, dark road to be choosing."

"My road, however, kind mother," said Shaina, "and you know it."

"And is your heart strong and your will like an oak?"

"Stronger. Test me. Or maybe the Grey Lady thinks I have been tested already and not found wanting."

Barbayat looked at Shaina with her knife-edge eyes; Shaina looked at Barbayat, and Barbayat read her.

"Once, chains of metal," said Barbayat, "now other chains. Still a slave. Listen then, love's slave, and hear and remember. I shall be speaking of Volkhavaar, his history. I do not tell you twice."

The road was long and hard; it took a day to regain Arkev, as Barbayat had said. But how good to feel the rough bitter stones under two human soles, the stormy wind harsh in two human eyes, and on a young girl's face and tugging at her hair. How good.

The black mountains of cloud never shifted from the horizon of Shaina's path. They might have been built over Arkev ten million years before. Yet, as she came nearer, she saw the purple and the garnet tufts caught in the valleys and rifts of them: the evidence of lamps and fires.

Very often the dark god was honored now: such was

Volk's decree. When the lights burned bright with that brackish glare, then it was such a time.

Shaina never paused. Her feet kept on walking. But her heart shuddered against her breast, deserts possessed her mouth, and she was very cold. But fear was like a dog to her now, an unreasonable companion. She was well used to fear. Sometimes she might throw him a bone, or pat his head to still him, but he would not stop her returning to the city, that grey whiner at her heel.

Presently, long after sunset—if sunset had shown its flame, which it did not—she reached the outskirts of Arkev, the walls, the river with its shipping, the towers and wide streets. All were black, as she remembered, but here and there flushed with torches.

The words of Barbayat rang in her mind, and Shaina clenched her teeth on that crust of resolution, that bread of destiny the witch had given her along with the other actual loaf.

The aura of the magician was everywhere, but never mind.

'I am alive,' she thought, 'he has not beaten me yet.'

Woana sat before her jewel casket.

Her eyes were blank as stones, and her heart blank with miserable, unalleviated fright.

No one could save her. She could not save herself. There was to be no escape. Volkhavaar held her in his power, amused by her symbolic worth. He had slain her hapless, foolish parents and turned Arkev over to sunless devilry and horror, and she must sit by. Sit with him, even. Sit watching in the Temple when the frenzied people worshipped Sovan Tovannazit with their orgies and beastliness, while her blood-wedded husband sat close, coldly devouring the spectacle with a dreadful, impossibly objective triumph.

She knew the people, her people, could not help what they did, were as much in his power as she was. She knew that unspeakable things happened after—the great, black wolf which stole through the streets and tore out the throats of revellers. One day the wolf might enter this chamber. . . .

There was no one she could turn to. Even her cat seemed bewitched, sometimes running from him as if driven to do so against her will, then nestling under his abominable caressing palms. Her Mitz, purring on the knee of Volkhavaar.

Now had come another message from her lord that she must go with him in his chariot, through the tumultuous city, into the Temple, and she could not bear it.

Something had happened to Woana. Something which should happen subtly and gently but seldom does. Something which in her had occurred with the stroke of an iron axe cleaving her inoffensive life in two. She had grown up. She was a woman. A woman, prey to an ultimate in terror, and after all, too proud and too strong to suffer her own timidity and weakness at such an hour.

In a jewel box, once loaded with the rare and fabulous gifts of her sinister bridegroom, lay one long-bladed pin. Woana, white as flax, was gazing at this pin, and her heart was ice already, waiting for the silver point to impale it.

Out stole her hand, like a thief through a shadow, trying not to let her see where it was going. On the pearl hilt of the pin her fingers fastened. She took it up and held it near her and shut her eyes tight.

Scratch, went something on the window pane. Scratch, scratch.

Woana dropped her makeshift dagger with a cry, and spun about.

"Mitz!" she exclaimed, running to the window.

Outside, the blackness hid everything, even the vile and occult colors of the glass.

Woana flung open the window before she had even thought, and instead of four, soft, slippery-silk paws and a furry serpent's head with ears, strong slim girl's hands grasped hers and a girl's voice said quickly: "Don't be afraid, Princess. I shan't harm you. Trust me and let me in before my foot slips and I fall back into the garden below."

Woana disengaged her hands and stepped aside, allowing access to the room. Unmistakably the visitor was human, and somehow had a curious conviction and sense of purpose to it conveyed instantaneously through grasp and voice. Woana found herself reassured rather than troubled as a maiden with raven hair, and dressed like the poorest of all the poor, swung nimbly into the chamber. Lovely the girl was, too, Woana noted, but, in her extremity, the old shyness failed to master her.

"Please tell me how you came to the window," said she,

however, striving to be at home with the unlooked-for situation.

"A wild way, madam: shinning a torch pole, over a wall, along a lawn, up a tree on to some stonework, to the window ledge. A cat's way up, and taught me by a cat. I beg your pardon, but there is not much time."

"Time for what?" questioned Woana, apprehending somehow, dimly, that fate was near at hand, and represented by this magnetic girl, who seemed oddly familiar and yet unknown.

"You must go with Volk, as before, must you not? And surely the Princess is unwilling to go to the Temple and worship the black one there? Or maybe I presume. Maybe she relishes such an evening."

"No, oh, no!" burst out Woana. "I would rather die, I would rather—"

"Indeed, but no special need for you to die, madam, when I am willing to take your place."

"You?"

"I."

At this the princess's legs betrayed her and she sat down unsteadily, and stared.

"Why—?" she whispered.

"Why not? I have business to settle with Volk Volkhavaar, wrecker of lives and cities." And the girl laughed, clear as crystal, surprising both Woana and, as it seemed, herself.

Shaina's fear had gone out of her in a rush, that dog no longer yapping at her heels. Now she felt exhilarated, tense as a bow-string, yet able, ready, certain. She felt her fate, as Woana had felt it on her, with a kind of witch-sight, and a humble pride.

"I think," Shaina said, "I am about your height and we are neither of us fat. Probably you would loan me a dress and a veil, not for vanity, the Princess will understand, but for purposes of disguise."

Woana gazed at her. Yes, it might be done, though Shaina was slender for her own thinness, a young willow by her own bony body.

"I will do whatever you want. But why do you want these things?"

"Heaven protect me, to try to finish Volkhavaar."

Woana bit her lips, then turned and flung wide the

closet doors as, not so long since, the ill-starred Duchess, her mother, had flung them.

"Take my wedding dress, which is gold, and a veil of gold embroidery to go with it."

"The finest I ever wore," said Shaina, "I thank you."

At another time, she might have lingered, having put on the dragon-scale gown and nipped in the waist with a girdle of blue fires, and having netted her hair in gilt and gems, she might have drunk her reflection from the burnished mirror, she who had rarely seen herself and never in comparable garments. But tonight such dreams were behind her. Other dreams, too, perhaps. She was altered, a girl no longer, only a creature all of Will and Intention.

Woana lowered her eyes briefly before the apparition, scorched by its magnificence. Then the tinselly veil fell over the face and concealed it.

"No," said Woana, "I don't walk that way. I creep, with my head drooping and my shoulders stooped." She said it factually, shamelessly.

Shaina bowed.

"Do so no longer, noble lady. When I have gone, you go too, south, out of Arkev. Make good your escape."

"I don't know how you hope to win your battle—or even what your battle is," said Woana, "but if you win it, I think I needn't fly. If you lose, I shan't be safe from him. So I shall stay. Are you a sorceress?"

"I pray I am. We shall see. Now tell me, will he knock?"

"No. When the next bell strikes, I must go down to him. *You* must go down to him. He will ride in a great, black chariot through the streets to the Temple. The horses of the chariot are black, their mouths flame. In the Temple you must sit beside him, and then—"

"And then," said Shaina. "I know, having seen it. But tonight it will be different."

A sound came through the city, a sound followed by another sound. The first, a noise of bells, the second, a noise of shouts, cries, a raucous chanting.

"I will be going," said Shaina.

"Will the night end soon?" asked Woana, briefly reverting, a child in the dark.

"All nights," said Shaina, "end."

And in her weird glory, moving differently now, a replica of Woana, Shaina opened the door, and went out and down the stairway.

To where he waited. Volkhavaar.

The last occasion she had seen him she had been in Mitz's body, had felt the glamour of his hands. But before that he had been her demon, the blackness which pursued her, hunted her, left her to her death; the shadowless shadow which lay over the one she loved, her only love.

And now, what? Would fear sweep up over her at this sight of him, his long face, his claws, his mouth and wolf teeth.

No. No fear. She had her own armor. If it was not strong enough, the armor, she would presently die, but oh, she would be ready for that even.

And when she thought of Dasyel, she no longer thought of him as a man, a lover, a dream. He also had become a symbol, though she did not recognize this bizarre fact at that fraught moment of her life.

"My wife is prompt," said Volkhavaar. "Perhaps tonight she is eager to join in the festivities? It can be arranged."

Shaina shuddered, shivered, trembled, as Woana would have done, as she had seen Woana do when she had observed her through Mitz's eyes.

Volk led her out.

The black city was feverish, hectic with fires of unnatural shades—crimson madder, violet, brown and brass. Fireworks flashed lividly in the sky. The black chariot stood waiting—so like the chariot he had hunted her in with his lupine head grinning, terror beyond reason and beyond enduring—but not the same chariot. An illusion. Volk handed her in.

A whip of green lightning gnashed and sizzled. A chain of women, half-naked, screaming like animals pierced by spikes, running behind, black priests moaning, a smell of perfume and corruption. Flowers grown from the darkest soil of soul and mind.

"I see you have honored me by putting on your wedding dress," said the magician to her, "and veiled yourself. Well, never mind. I suspect Arkev will survive without the vision of your beauty."

Shaina cowered beside him, and Volk stretched his lips. As once before, he suspected nothing, was blind to the Omen, deaf to the Knell. It was love had destroyed him before, but he had forgotten it.

They came to the Sun Court and the steps. They rode straight up the steps and into the Temple, and the people ran to keep near, whooping and laughing.

Torches roared in ranks of purple stars.

The four-faced god, a tower of eyes and hunger, touching the roof with his head.

Shaina looked at him. Her pulses drummed, and the surge of her veins and arteries strangled her, yet still it was not fear, and could never be fear again. She had gone too far and too fast for fear to catch her.

She looked about. She saw Dasyel, Yevdora, Roshi. The black priests swarmed about the defiled altar. A black horse had mounted on it, and stood there like basalt. The air was charged with power and waiting.

Volkhavaar pulled her from the chariot, and strode towards his god, and the people yelled and fell to their knees on either side. Volk did not notice how she no longer walked in Woana's fashion, how her stride matched his.

"Takerna," cried Volk.

And the whole Temple echoed back: "Takerna, Takerna, the Black One, the Lord of Night and Shadowed Places!"

And the torches leaped, the black horse leaped; the moment poised on the brink of the future. And:

"Wait, my Beloved Husband," said a soft little voice at Volkhavaar's side. "I, too, wish to worship the greatest god of Arkev."

Volk, letting go of her wrist, turned to look at her. He guessed the difference now, but could not resolve it. She was not Woana, but *who was* she?

"You are proud," said the veiled woman, still in a cool, quiet tone, "of your hard life, your struggle, the pain and waiting and the death from which you emerged to become what finally you are, Volk Volkhavaar, Kernik, Prophet of the God. I, too, have known pain and struggle and a grave. I, too, have given blood. I, too, have changed my shape. I, too, have risen from death in the morning. We are like brother and sister, you and I, O magician, out of one womb. Both outlanders, both orphans, both slaves, both freed of chains, both striving and strong of will, and both with our own abilities, matched yet dissimilar."

Volk paused. All Arkev felt him pause. He said:

"Unveil yourself."

And the woman bowed, and lifted her hands, unfastened the veil and let it fall.

"My name is Shaina," she said. "You told me once you did not need to know. Perhaps you have altered your opinion. You watched them sever my head and my soul fade. Yet here I am, whole as you see, come back from Death's country as you did, Volk Volkhavaar."

Volk faltered. All Arkev felt him falter. He raised his arm. Shaina said:

"Your magic is illusion. Don't try illusion on this girl you see here. She'll laugh at you. She won't believe in your devils, your black horses, your wolf's face. She's survived them."

Volk spoke then. A voice of serpents. It said, as might have been expected, only one word, one name: *"Takerna."*

Inky light swooped across the Temple, doused the pillars, flattened the torches burning now with grey flames.

Shaina turned. She went swiftly and set her hands on the blood stained feet of the huge statue. No longer did she glance at Volk. She looked upwards, upwards into that cruel, unhuman face above her.

"Not Takerna," said Shaina quietly. "Sovan Tovannazit. Once, on a mountain, they named you for the shadow and the dark rock and the pines below. And a boy came there. He sensed the faint spirit, all that was left of you. He worshipped you and entreated you with all the strength in him, all the strength of his hate and his violence. And you answered, you returned. You fed on hatred and on blood, and you grew. He gave you his life and you became his life. You ate his shadow and the shadows of those three beside the altar."

The air flickered and throbbed.

"Maiden," said Volkhavaar, "the river is very black and very wide. How are you thinking you will get across it?"

"Magician," said Shaina, "the river is wide, but shallow. Shallow enough for a child to get across it. Watch, and you shall see how it is done." Then she stood back from the statue. She raised her arms. She called out in a voice as passionate and barbaric as any Kernik or Volk had ever used: "Sovan Tovannazit, High Lord, Wind Lord. *He* forgets, but your servant does not. *I* am your true priestess and I return to worship you as it befits you to be worshipped. But not with black blood, not with human sacrifice." And she drew out of her breast the white flowers the witch had

plucked, still magically whole, and laid them on the feet of
the god, and bending, kissed the place where she had laid
them.

The light in the Temple seethed as if full of bats' wings.

Volkhavaar stood watching. He said:

"Do you think you can fight me, then, slave girl with
the lovesick heart?"

"Fight you?" said Shaina, turning back, leaning on the
feet of the statue. "I can destroy you, magician. Which
rules, night or day, day or night? Equal they are, and one
must give place to the other. Men make gods in the image
of themselves. All it needs is passion, Volkhavaar. My passion is as great as yours. You hate to the limit of your
flesh and brain, you would die for your hate and so hate
is your god; I love to the limit of my flesh and brain, and
I would die for my love. What god do I make? That is my
white shield negating your black sword, my white sword
that cleaves your black shield. Sovan," she said, her eyes
shining, and she began to speak the ancient ritual that
Kernik had learned from the priest so many unrecorded
years before in the village of pine logs. Barbáyat, looking
into her crystal at Volk's past, had missed nothing. She
was a good teacher and Shaina an excellent pupil. Performed fully, the ritual was a long one, but Shaina did not
leave out a single phrase. And when it was done, she borrowed again from the words the yellow boy had uttered on
the mountain. Only she said it this way:

"Great Lord Sovan, I have done all as it should be
done. I will raise you up and make you a god again, a
mighty god to be adored and honored throughout the
Korkeem and the lands that lie thigh by thigh with her. But
in order that I may do this, you in return must grant me
some power. Gift for gift, Unconquerable One. Disgorge
those souls you took. You no longer need them, High
Lord, Wind Lord, *White* Lord, Lord of Day and Shadowless Places. For you are not a god of hate, you are a white
god of solar disc and lunar orb and cloudless sky: the pure
god of the wine-horn, the harvest, the white horse. *This* is
what you are, and that darkness there only the shade cast
sideways from the vast pearly light of you, like a shadow
from the sun. You have been honored wrongly. Now, I do
it right."

Then it came, leaving her—for she felt it leave her like

the pang of birth or the tumble into death—a huge, warm, pulsing emotion, goodness, innocence and delight. Her tears were falling on the black stone. Her tears said: "Kill me if you wish, I consent, only let me be the last, not the first." She was prepared to die to end death, as the mother gives herself to the bear in order that her child may escape. That is the raging, stupid, arcane and primitive nature of love, thrusting all before it like the sea. It is hate which is rational, hate which makes laws. Love does not need them. Love *knows*.

But Shaina did not die, only she felt the virtue go out of her, fierce and weakening as any blood. She saw her tears wash the filth and stains from the idol's feet, wash them and wash them, leaving a black stone which was, in turn, washed to a grey stone, which in turn again, grew white as salt.

And, looking up through her crying, that great mass of a god was towering like a silver pillar, no longer falcon-masked, and with a gentle hand, the ivory horn in it wanting only wine or clear water.

A wind blew. It blew the black light in the Temple to shreds, it rent the miasma like curtains.

The crowd was weeping, like children waking from a nightmare, without horror or self-reproach, with thankfulness. There was a luminous mist streaming and piercing through their ranks. It struck with milky, golden notes on pillars, on the gorgeous windows, on the red robes of the priests. On the white horse it struck, standing like marble beside the altar, struck also on the holy altar cloth, pristine as snow with a fringe of untarnished bullion. It struck on Roshi, the fat man, who was cursing in an execrable, merry way; on Dasyel, the young actor, who, with his eyes wide open, was cursing in much the same manner, looking about and putting an arm around Yevdora who, twisting her yellow hair over her fingers, was saying bewilderedly:

"Where are the water pitchers? I shall be home late!"

"Home late you will be indeed," said Roshi, "some months late, or years maybe."

While through the Temple doors the source of the light was swelling the color of roses and molten topaz, a dawn worth seeing, and the sun returning with it into Arkev.

And against those burning skies, all the white towers, the glistening domes, the bright ships on the river, and

Woana running out of the pale palace, meeting there a small, black cat and dancing with it, and the sun painting her face better than any cosmetic, making her almost pretty.

✻ 22 ✻

The power of Volk's black god was over, finished. It could never come back, for love had changed it, love as strong as hate, as resolute, as ruthless, and love would keep that power white as it kept white the image. Volk's kingdom had fallen once again. Before, it had been the youth tumbling to his death, dragging the darkness with him, shattering it. But now it was the maiden, kissing Death on his cold cheek, banishing Night for good, simply by calling it Day. She too was mistress of illusion, conjuror of souls; she was all she had said; the magician's sister with the sorcery of her tears and her open, savage heart. Even the dark stone on the magician-showman's staff, that fragment of Takerna himself, was pale now as a pearl.

Kernik had wept that first time, snivelled in abject fear, feeling the greatness ebb from him. This time, like a man suddenly missing all his limbs, he strove blindly, frantically, to clothe himself, to make an illusion. And the ability was mute. Either because his god was no longer his, or merely because he had no true confidence to be master without his own master's cloak thrown over him.

He turned about, snarling, facing one way, then another way, defying, baring his teeth, like a mad dog, but only a man. Only that.

He was dressed in wisps of things, rags of the plain, poor reality over which he had constructed the robes of his splendor, fooling everybody, even himself.

If they attacked him now, these people, attacked him as they would always attack the toppled colossus, he could defend himself with nothing. No wolf shape to rend them, no falcon wings to bear him into that sky of dawn rinsing the storm from the city.

He circled about. He wanted to lick his wounds, to run, to be safe, to howl and beat his hands on the rocks. He did not know his age, could not reckon it, but he was an adolescent again, broken and helpless before them in the snow under the peak.

And the spell had dropped from them. Vengeance would be warming their frozen veins. Hands creeping to knives, groping for stones, as before.

Could he die? Could they kill him? No—somehow he sensed that, at least, was left to him, the uncertain span he had received in return for blood and soul. And he continued to cast no shadow, unlike the three minions he had kept in bondage so long. The witch called Shaina had returned *their* souls, the souls which Volk had snatched from them. Only his, given voluntarily, and obliterated, could not be reclaimed. And those three, what would they be doing? The girl Yevdora wept, Roshi grinned, bemused. The young actor, however, standing arrogant, cool, knowing him, knowing him perfectly and what had been done. Dasyel did not take kindly to his slavery. He was looking for a sword, clearly wondering if his fists would do, eyes level as blue-green ice on the raddled face of the shrinking magician—

Volk turned. Volk ran. Fright and agony and despair bit and gashed him. He howled, as he wanted, like a wolf. He burst from the Temple, through the streets. His impetus, his maniac wailing got him past the excited crowds, who presently, however, ran after him.

He was not so quick, any more, not so limber, all his agility gone in chains and dungeons aeons since.

Somehow, no one caught him. Perhaps they loathed the idea of touching him. And maybe, on that day of the white god, Sovan Tovannazit, they could not bring themselves to strike blows of hate.

He reached the river Karga. He was insane and gouged to his bones. He plunged into it, he who had been the pike, king of fish, who had swum and hunted deep in the deep green waterlands; Volk the man thought he would drown or burn, was not sure which, as the river closed over him, stifled him, sped up in bubbles to the surface and met the small pebbles and rotten fruits the people of Arkev flung in after him.

He never heard the cry when it rose, rose with pigeons and tuneful bells to greet the sun:

"The black beast is *dead, dead, dead!*"

Arkev, too, was free from her chains.

The time of all slaves was past.

And after all this, a silence. And in the silence, things to be settled.

Potters make pots with each side even, but life does not do so.

Woana, the plain princess, now Duchess of Arkev with her cat purring exclusively once again on her knees, who would ever have thought she would have got one husband, let alone two. In the months to come, someone she once shyly liked and would have trusted, a brown fat man, player of tunes, friend of babies and sparrows, will become what he never dreamed he would be: Duke of the Korkeem, Woana's husband.

At first he will have looked at her and seen only a dull little girl. He will have felt sorry for her, and so tried to cheer her up, always his way, Roshi, the ever kind. Then he will have seen how she blossomed under his kindness, seen other things too. Her own kindness, her humbleness, her surprising thoughtfulness for her people in the white city, for, now she had grown up, she has made a resolve never to rule foolishly, as her father did, or wickedly as did Volkhavaar. She had learnt some useful lessons. And when one day Roshi will discover he likes her company more than any other's—rather the way he has always liked to sit with a small bird whose wing he has mended, watching it getting well and happy, he will see her look at him, and things will be arranged. Roshi will say to Woana: "I can't marry a Duchess. Give it up and come and live with me in a cottage," and Woana will say: "I must stay and consider my people," and her head will be held high as Shaina's. So Roshi will have to agree to be a Duke, which will ultimately make little difference except to certain ambassadors from foreign parts marvelling at the Duke's musical talents, and the amazing juggling turns he puts on at dinner. And when there has been a crib or two filled, Woana will say to him, "Beloved Husband," and mean it. "Tell me," she will say, "why you ever wanted me, I am so plain and dull." And Roshi will say: "No one notices the nightingale till it sings." And anyone who looks closely then at Woana will in any case see she is no longer plain or dull at all.

That is Roshi and Woano.

As for Yevdora, she will go home and marry a safe, hardworking man, which is quite inevitable, if unenterprising of her. Really, despite her loveliness, only Volk's

magic had made her interesting. She will be content at
home in Yevdor with her loom, her children and her un-
sorcerous spouse, and who can blame her?

And thus almost to the last turn of the wheel, and the
clay which began it; the slave girl and her actor. And for
that the spin must stay at that first, fresh dawn in Arkev
when the magician fled.

In the silence which folded over Arkev, birds could be
heard singing high up in the sky, little bells, ringing to the
sun.

Everyone was gone from the Temple—the people, even
the priests gone to greet the morning—all but two. The
Temple was white, washed clean, and the vast, gentle god
stood in his whiteness, still as sleep.

And beneath him stood Shaina, and about five paces
from her stood Dasyel. And they looked at each other,
steady and seeing, unabashed and truthful, at last.

If she had confronted him like this all that while before,
when first she loved him, she could not have gazed so
calmly, straight in his eyes, those eyes that pierced her
heart. She would have had to tremble and to look down
with her emotion hard as rock in her throat. But now
things had come between, strange things, stranger even
than the spell the magician laid on him. So she could look
and she could see, and there was no doubt.

Barbayat had told her she would know, and know she
did. In his eyes were admiration, liking, desire even, but
not love, not love like hers. And she comprehended how
such a love as hers, meeting less than itself, would devour
him and mutilate her, and so it was.

Then Dasyel, the nobleman's son, the actor, bowed to
her beautifully, and he said:

"I think the young lady is a witch? May I know her
name to thank her, for I imagine I understand what she
has done for me."

"My name is Shaina," said Shaina, "by your leave. And
yours Dasyel. So much I have learned."

But he had been looking in her eyes too, and he had
seen her mind as she had seen his. He came a pace closer,
and graciously and low he said to her:

"The young lady who is a witch called Shaina knows I
am forever in her debt. She is very beautiful and very

clever, and if she would consider accepting me as her husband, I should be exceptionally honored."

"You," said Shaina, even more softly than he, "would be exceptionally foolish. It is foolish, you see, for so intelligent a young man to be taking as his wife one he does not love."

Dasyel regarded her a minute or more. He said:

"I am thinking it would be easy enough to grow to love you, Shaina."

"And I am thinking," said Shaina, "that I loved you without growing to it, that you are my only love, that I will never love another. I am not ashamed to tell you this. There is no shame in loving and never was. Neither do I reproach you that your eyes did not answer mine. It is something that cannot be helped. I have worn enough chains that I never wished to chain up others. Your road, I hazard, is as it always was, and I can't travel it with you. Go free, Dasyel, you owe me nothing. Do we offer the grain payment when it ripens, or the moon when it rises? I could do no other than I did."

After which she smiled at him, for the sadness in her was not of the sort which makes smiling impossible. She went a little closer to him and touched his curling hair with one finger.

"I have heard them say that those with curly hair have curly thoughts. You had best be careful of that on the road."

And then, still smiling, she turned and she walked away towards the Temple door. And Dasyel called after her:

"Maybe we shall meet later on, Shaina the witch."

"If you need me, seek me, I will help you. If you can find me, I will be waiting. There will never be another, and if you return to me I shall be glad. But I won't grieve for you or look for you, Dasyel. May the sun shine on you always, and goodbye."

So she took her road, and he his. His road was the old one, the actors' road, the way of rain and hard beds, the way of the painted carts, the princes in starry armor, the lovers, the brawls, the land forever changing. Her road ended at Barbayat's door, and began there too. Not idly did they call Shaina sorceress after that. That was the crown she had guessed at, the way that claimed her, which, through her love, she had never before noted, as the earth itself is seldom noted under its mantle of soil and grass, though it is there, and never doubt it. The irony of her story is merely that her love became, in the end, her motive rather than her goal, the doorway rather than the house.

And perhaps one day, in any case, someone came walking up Barbayat's mountain, or some other mountain where Barbayat was and her apprentice-daughter, someone with black, curling hair, thinking of Shaina as once she had thought of him. Who knows?

For all things alter, nothing is certain.

Who dares say, for example, that that toppling of the magician was his last toppling? On some muddy bank, far downstream of the Karga, envisage some man-fish washed ashore, Kernik Volk, no longer Volkhavaar, staring about, cold as hate, starting again his gurning war with the Korkeem and with men.

For day follows night, night day; then comes day again. The apples ripen, the apples fall, the birds peck them, seeds drop from their beaks—and somewhere new apple trees begin to grow. That is how it is, a circle, a ring. And the world turns.